# Recipe for Eagle Cove

## a small town Oregon romance

by

M. L. Buchman

Discover more by this author at:
www.mlbuchman.com

Cover images:
Couple In Love Walking On A Beautiful Autumn Alley In
The Park Photo © Peshekhonova | Dreamstime.com

Buchman Bookworks

# Other works by M. L. Buchman:

### Angelo's Hearth
*Where Dreams are Born*
*Where Dreams Reside*
*Maria's Christmas Table*
*Where Dreams Unfold*
*Where Dreams Are Written*

### Eagle Cove
*Return to Eagle Cove*
*Recipe for Eagle Cove*

### The Night Stalkers
*The Night Is Mine*
*I Own the Dawn*
*Daniel's Christmas*
*Wait Until Dark*
*Frank's Independence Day*
*Peter's Christmas*
*Take Over at Midnight*
*Light Up the Night*
*Christmas at Steel Beach*
*Bring On the Dusk*
*Target of the Heart*
*Target Lock on Love*
*Christmas at Peleliu Cove*
*Zachary's Christmas*
*By Break of Day*

### Firehawks
*Pure Heat*
*Wildfire at Dawn*
*Full Blaze*
*Wildfire at Larch Creek*
*Wildfire on the Skagit*
*Hot Point*
*Flash of Fire*

### Delta Force
*Target Engaged*

### Deities Anonymous
*Cookbook from Hell: Reheated*
*Saviors 101*

### Thrillers
*Swap Out!*
*One Chef!*
*Two Chef!*

### SF/F Titles
*Nara*
*Monk's Maze*

# Chapter 1

$A$*n air of delighted* mischief pervaded the room as Becky and Natalya changed out of their bridesmaids dresses. Jessica Baxter had always sworn she would never marry. Instead she was the first of the three friends to go down…and they were going to make her pay for being so fortunate.

Becky peered out the second-story window; it was easy to pick Jessica out of the crowd which spread across the B&B's broad lawn. The stately Victorian stood well back from the high bluff above the rolling Pacific. The bride was long, blond, sleek, and gorgeous in a simple white lace gown. The Sunday afternoon sun of the warm September day—because *of course* it wouldn't dare rain on Jessica's wedding—sparkled off her as if she was half elf and half fairy. Both of which Becky had always suspected to be true.

And Becky couldn't begrudge one of her best friends getting Greg Slater because the two were so perfect together. But she could be envious. And the only proper way to deal with envy was merry revenge.

She couldn't suppress her giggle as they were changing. Natalya flashed a grin back at her; Jessica's first cousin was like the anti-Jessica. The two of them were both tall and slim, but Natalya was dusky-skinned, brunette, and had all of the curves that Jessica had whined about not having since forever. It had been Natalya's idea for them to change into little black dresses for the wedding reception, as if they were mourning Jessica's demise. Pure pixie, always a tricky lot, Natya was the strategist of their childhood trio.

Becky had fashioned matching corsages for them out of black tissue paper. Those dozen years of schooling had finally paid off, even if it was just in crafts projects from the first grade. She preferred the down and dirty school of hard knocks that had spanned the last fourteen years since graduating from Puffin High.

She turned back to the room and saw that she had another problem. Natalya in a little black dress was going to gobsmack every man around and Becky didn't think that was much more fair than Jessica looking so ridiculously happy.

Becky checked herself in the mirror, not that it did her much good. Natalya lived three hours away in Portland, so she was staying in the Writer's Room of her mother's Victorian B&B. It was an airy, lofty-ceilinged room typical of the old architecture. This room was filled with books, images of writers, and the décor was pure Jane Austen-era Georgian. That meant that the mirror had a massively ornate, gold-painted frame. Yet despite its imposing presence, it was actually small, round, and set far too high for Becky's five-four. That her two best friends since kindergarten were both five-ten was just another injustice. What she'd lacked in stature she'd made up for in curves, "lush Italianate curves" her similarly-shaped mother had always said—which made perfect sense with their pioneer-stock, Gold-Rush era, boringly Anglo-Saxon heritage. Not!

She was… Becky had never been able to pin down what she was. Imp? Garden gnome? The right metaphor always eluded her. She sighed, standing on tiptoe didn't help either.

Unable to see her reflection much below the generous cleavage that even the most conservative little black dress gave a woman of her shape—and this dress was not meant to be conservative—she turned for help.

"Your mom's stupid mirrors. Help me, Natya!" It was an old problem that didn't need explaining.

Natalya whirled a finger and Becky did a turn on the ornate Persian rug that looked as if it had been snatched out of the Hogwarts Gryffindor Common Room, making the bedroom warm and cozy. J. K. Rowling watched Becky from her portrait over Natalya's shoulder. Emily Dickinson considered one profile and Jane Austen the other. Maya Angelou may have been inspecting her shoes. She'd pulled on her bright red cowboy boots with the pretty black stitching. The low heel was good because of dancing on the lawn. Besides, Becky held a firm conviction that high heels on a short woman were just a lame form of sucking up. And whatever James Tiptree, Jr. was thinking about Becky's shoulder-length auburn hair, she was keeping to herself, just as she'd kept her gender hidden through two decades of writing science fiction. Georgette Heyer merely hung on the wall and looked magnificently 1920s as she always did.

Natalya shot out a thumbs up. "Men are going to whimper!"

"Yes!" Becky offered a fist pump and did a little circular stomp dance on the rug. "That is if they notice me with you around."

"Since when have you ever had to worry about that?"

"Since Jessica looks so damn happy dancing with Greg." Together they turned to look back out the window. Becky half wanted to collect the writers' pictures from the walls so that all the women in the room could look out together.

"It *is* a little like she's bragging, isn't it?"

Becky could only nod. Jessica was draped shamelessly against her new husband, slow dancing to an up-tempo Backstreet Boys song. Three months ago Jessica returned to Eagle Cove after a decade working as a Chicago journalist. She was supposed to be here just a week and then return to her whirlwind urban career.

Instead, she'd stayed as the town's new marketing manager and was kicking ass at it. Tourism was at its highest level in years. That was good news for the Lamont's B&B, the real estate business of Jessica's mom, and it certainly hadn't hurt Becky's brewery.

"Time to go break up all of this unmitigated happiness." Natya declared firmly. It was. And Jessica was right, Natalya was always the sneaky one of the group.

"First dibs on cutting in on the bride for a dance with the groom," Becky declared just as Natalya was opening her mouth to do the same.

"Damn!" Natalya's curse warmed her heart.

To secure her victory, Becky raced for the door, offered an air high-five to Nora Roberts' picture above an entire bookcase filled with her writings, and beat Natalya to the stairs. But she was blockaded from escape at the bottom of the stairs…the kitchen was packed. She was in the midst of the mayhem, when across the impenetrable mob, she saw Natalya slink down the old servants' back stairs and out onto the porch. Her wicked grin showed exactly where she was headed—to claim the second dance from the groom.

"Damn!" All she could do was echo Natalya's heartfelt curse of a moment before. Becky stomped her foot in frustration; growing up in this house gave Natalya an unfair advantage.

# # #

Harry yelped more in surprise than pain as someone tromped on the toes of his Oxfords. The kitchen was so noisy with a dozen simultaneous conversations that no one particularly noticed his cry. It took him a moment to spot his attacker, but when he looked down he discovered an astonishing sight.

The first thing he noticed was the impressive swell of exposed breasts. It wasn't that they were all that uncovered, they were just very…impressive. *Ah yes, his lawyerly finesse with words. Sad.* But it was hard to be completely coherent when faced with such an exceptional view. Then he forced himself to focus on the owner's face.

"Becky!" He ignored her smirk that said she knew exactly where his attention had first landed and gave her quick hug that she returned after a moment. "It's like old home week." Everyone had turned out for his little brother's wedding. The fact that Greggie was marrying, *had* married, the first woman Harry had ever kissed didn't bother him…too much. He and Jess had been almost done before they started during freshman year. Wasn't it just backward justice that Greg was the one who'd always had the big crush on her without ever admitting to it.

"Old home week only to you foreign types." Becky Billings smirk had shifted to tease, something he recalled her excelling at. Her light brown eyes practically twinkled with delight. He also recalled that among other things, she'd absolutely ruled every class debate in high school. He might have ruled the soccer field, but her quick mind and quicker tongue had ruled the verbal playing field.

"Foreign as in a hundred yards down the road," he gave it his best shot. His family's homestead was the other grand Victorian of the town. The two old houses stood at the head of the beach and commanded the best views in Eagle Cove.

"Foreign as in you live in New Orleans and are just here slumming."

"Care to do a little slumming with me?"

"You call that a pickup line?" Becky snorted out a laugh and slapped him hard enough on the arm to send him ricocheting off Cal Mason Jr. who bumped into Cal Mason Sr. in earnest conversation with Jessica's father. Cal Sr. shoved Jr. back into him and the two of them ended up tangled together against the stove, both struggling not to spill their beers all over each other.

"Sorry, Cal, Becky just—" he pointed, but the spot where she'd been was empty. Cal gave him a look as if checking his mental capacity: low, after the view of Becky's chest had drained the blood out of his brain.

He looked around and caught occasional glimpses of the top of her head as she moved through the tight-packed kitchen crowd, her liquid-oak hair floating lightly behind her. The crowd parted just enough to offer him a full view as she stepped out the far door and onto the sunlit porch.

She might be short, barely up to his chin, but her industrial-grade curves and trim waist looked damn good on her. And that dress. *Holy wow!* Spaghetti shoulder straps, clinging material, and a flirty flare high enough on her thighs to reveal that there was no excess load on that frame. She was no runner, couldn't be with that body, but they were damned amazing legs. Then with a exuberant "Yip!" of excited greeting, loud enough that he could hear it over the music and the overlapping chatter, she raced out into the sunlight and was gone.

Harry rubbed his shoulder where she'd hit him. He'd forgotten how strong she was. He'd have to remember that the next time he caught up with her. And the way she looked, he definitely had some catching up to do. But he didn't want to appear overeager either. So, he leaned back against the stove with Cal. They'd been the forward strikers on the soccer team back at Puffin High, finishing the season ten-and-two, a new pinnacle for the Pufflings. Cal Sr. and his own father, Judge Slater, had chosen the ridiculous baby seabird as the school mascot most of half a century before. He'd never found out quite why, so he and Cal Jr. worked on their beers and rehashed it some for old times' sake.

But what he really wanted to talk about was Becky Billings and the way that woman looked in a clinging black dress with chili pepper red cowboy boots.

# # #

Becky snagged her dance with Greg once she'd dug Natalya's claws out of him. She did a turn with Vincent McCall while Greg danced with Vincent's wife Emily. Then after Becky twirled and giggled with Emily's twin girls, the three of them raided the wedding cake for second pieces and wolfed them down as if they were about to be caught for being naughty.

Becky and Natalya made sure to point out their black mourning frocks to Jessica at every chance and the damn woman just nodded, giggled—which oddly didn't looked ridiculous on a thirty-two year old woman—then sighed happily. The whole black-dress ploy would have been a complete waste of time except they were drawing the attention of every single male, even snaring a few of the married ones into receiving eye rolls from their spouses. She pitied the male of the species. Around women like the three of them, the male gender didn't stand a chance.

Throughout the reception Becky had been keeping a weather eye on eligible men as she moved back and forth across the lawn, up onto the big porch that wrapped around the house and was so crowded with merrymakers, and back out onto the lawn. The problem was that she knew these men too well. Mick, Zander, Alex…it really *was* like old home week.

It was one of the only drawbacks to a small town. Every man her age she'd either dated, hated, or just knew too much about to do either. How did you find a man like Vincent or Greg while living in a small town? She and Greg had even taken a test spin around the track a few times when he first returned to Eagle Cove, but he'd clearly been looking for something else, as was she. Now he'd found it, but she still hadn't.

Evening was settling over the yard. The sun was turning brilliant orange as it descended into the fog bank that so often lingered a few miles offshore. It had been a perfect day for a wedding. Probably one of their last warm and sunny days until next spring.

Already the older generation was drifting inside to pack the kitchen, the library, and the parlor. The evening chill was rolling in off the Pacific so she'd be headed that way soon. Little black dresses offered no defense against the night sea air.

Actually, she already was chilled, standing alone and watching the endless waves roll in and hammer down on the sandy beach far below. Deciding to retreat, she turned abruptly for the house and rammed her nose into the center of a broad chest.

"Was looking for you." Harry Slater. He looked nothing like his brother or his father. The Judge, as everyone called him, was a large, imposing man. Greg was lean and darkly handsome just like his mother had been.

Harry stood as tall as his father, a little broader than Greg, and as blond-haired and blue-eyed as his brother and father weren't. The last time she'd seen Harry was at his mother's funeral three years ago.

"Looking for me?" Why was he looking for her? And if he was, why hadn't he done it sooner? "Took your time, foreigner. Waiting until the dancing was done?"

"Saw you dancing before."

She liked his voice. It was low and smooth—more like a distant freight train than a rumbling diesel engine. He had the kind of deep voice in a lawyer that would make a jury want to trust him. And his accentless Oregon had picked up a hint of Southern-smooth from his years in the Big Easy.

"Can't imagine how I'd keep up with that."

"Like this," she slid up against him and wrapped her arms around his back. A jazz sax was playing somewhere in the distance. She wasn't really sure what had come over her; not that much champagne had passed her lips. Becky might run a brewery, but she drank very little even on major occasions like today. Maybe it was how gorgeous he looked in his gray designer suit. She'd never known she was a sucker for men in great suits.

Harry hesitated for a long moment before wrapping his hands slowly around her shoulders. She didn't have to really duck to lay her head on his chest. His chin rested lightly on her hair and she let herself be swept up in the moment.

Just a moment.

She was in the arms of a handsome, successful, single man. Lying against his chest with her eyes closed as he guided them about the lawn to a deliciously slow cadence.

It was magical.

It shouldn't be.

Harry was just the groom's brother at a wedding, but she could pretend that he really had sought her out.

And maybe she him.

As long as she was pretending, maybe this was what "magical" actually felt like in real life. The music slipped by and the world melted along with it.

A slow shiver slipped over her arms.

"You okay?" Harry whispered it against her hair.

"Um, I think so." Why didn't she know? "You?"

"Oh yeah," he said in one of those deeply satisfied male ways.

She pulled out of his arms enough to look up at him. Without her noticing, the sun had set…long enough ago to make his expression hard to see. They were alone near the high bluff above the beach. Harry had kept them away from the few remaining dancers and some of the younger kids running about with sparklers flaring bright in the falling darkness. Twinkle lights which hung from the lower branches of the towering Douglas firs near the house cast a soft glow over the remnants of the party.

To the north, two miles of white sand beach stretched off to where the Eagle River entered the Pacific. The lights of the town of Eagle Cove were sparkling to life. The very first stars were also putting in an appearance. The ocean had gone nearly black, only marked now by the steady whump of the waves landing on the long strand in a never-ending cascade, There was the smell of salt and the promise of a fresh, amazing world.

High above the south end of the beach, perched atop a rocky headland that blocked any view in that direction, Orca Head Light cast its bright beams out to sea. It was just possible to see the path of the automated light sweeping across the waves far below. When the fog rolled in, it was a dramatic sight.

Even at the moment it was fairly breathtaking.

Speaking of breathtaking, how long had she just been lost in Harry's arms?

Simple answer: too long. It had been forever since she'd gotten *lost* in a boy's arms. The last time had been back when boys were still *boys* and not patented and certified *men* like one Harry Slater.

"That was…" *Lovely* was too mundane, even worse, too predictable. "…kinda pleasant coming from a foreigner."

# # #

Harry groaned.

It had been a full half an hour that he had held Becky Billings—close. At first it had been friendly, cozy, and arousing as hell. Becky was a sweet package to cuddle with. When he held her, he knew that he was, without question, holding a woman. And she had abandoned herself to it, letting whatever parts of them come together to do just that. When she stepped back, he could feel the cold replace the warm outline of her upon his chest.

"I'm used to a different kind of woman."

"What? Standoffish ones? No, you don't have that problem, do you? Tall ones? Beautiful ones?" She bit off the last strangely.

"I'm used to ones that I don't accidentally speak my thoughts aloud to." That was a given.

"Objection: irrelevant. The court directs the counselor to please answer the original question."

Harry could only stare down at her in astonishment.

"Well?" Becky demanded, her tone completely proper for a disdainful judge.

He looked out to sea for along moment, listened to the breaking waves through three or four landings upon the beach, but found no better answer out there.

"Spit it out, Counselor Slater. Keep this up and I'll find you in contempt."

"Okay…" No woman had ever even thought to speak to him in his own language and Becky Billings, Eagle Cove's pint-sized brewmaster was doing exactly that and doing it well.

Then he caught the hint of her smile despite the darkness. Having fun with him, was she? Well, he wasn't a courtroom lawyer for no reason.

"Contempt, huh?" Harry crossed his arms. "What's the fine if I fail to comply? As a counselor I am honor bound to protect the reputation of—"

"—of all the hot women you've bedded. Well," she crossed her own arms to mimic his position, which only emphasized the magnificence of her chest. "I will offer the counselor a choice of two options to offset the charge of contempt."

"Proceed." This had to be the strangest conversation he'd ever had with a woman that he'd—

Except he hadn't.

All they'd done was dance. No date, no drinks, no…well, none of that either.

"Your first option, Counselor, is a sharp poke in the ribs for being an over-confident, self-assured, *foreign* interloper."

He remembered how hard she'd hit his shoulder. "Not my first choice." Besides, if she did that, he just might tumble off the cliff and it was a long and very steep way down to the beach from the Lamont B&B. The access stairs were twenty or more paces to the north on the line between the Lamont and the Slater properties. Probably too far to make a break for it.

"Second option, pay the fine."

"The fine? Perhaps I should opt for the sharp poke in the ribs after all."

"Your call: answer the question about what type of women you're used to, a sharp poke, or pay the fine. The court has ruled."

He was having a very hard time not smiling. The muscles tugging at the corners of his mouth felt unfamiliar. There hadn't been a great deal to smile about lately in his life. It was almost as if he'd forgotten how, but Becky was rapidly reminding him.

She offered no clue as to what "the fine" might constitute.

But he most certainly wasn't going to answer her question about available women. His looks and his job did indeed make picking up women a simple task; he was never alone on a night he didn't want to be. Though lately he'd spent far more nights alone than with someone. He hadn't really noticed it until this moment. He wasn't bored with the sex, but there had been nothing special about it lately either.

"Well," he had to tease her a little, "I'll admit that you aren't as tall as most women who I've…"

He managed to dodge that poke in the ribs as much by luck and darkness as by light-footedness. Her laugh was awfully merry for a judge on the bench. Didn't he just know it. His father, Judge Slater, had never in his life spoken an unnecessary word to his wife or either of his sons.

"What the hell, why not. Okay, Judge Becky Billings, I'll take the fine. Nothing risked, nothing gained."

"My thoughts exactly."

# # #

Becky stepped forward until she was once again pressed against Harry Slater's splendid body. The yard had emptied while they'd sparred. They now owned the entire bluff from house to ocean.

Then she had a crazy, dumb idea after she was already stepping into his arms. She'd thought to cop another dance…

The man had been arrogant, a long time ago back in high school. But not any longer. It was as clear as the night sky that *that* had been kicked out of him somewhere along the road since he'd left town. He also wasn't happy, and that wasn't right.

Some trifecta of pity, a little champagne, and just how wonderfully he'd held her collided. Reaching up, she pulled him down to her and kissed him hard.

As she'd expected, a man who looked like Harry Slater had found plenty of opportunity to hone his kissing skills as well as his lawyering skills. As a matter of fact—she wished to hell she had worn spike stilettos with high platforms so that she could get closer to his kiss—if he was as good a lawyer as a kisser, he must be a kajillionaire.

His hands didn't wander much. Most men went for her breasts and never looked back. Harry wrapped one arm around her waist and the other around her shoulders and pulled her in until her feet were light in her boots.

He was foreign. His sharp gray suit that smelled…well, she wasn't sure, but it definitely wasn't Eagle Cove. He'd been the snappiest dressed man in the entire wedding, discounting only Greg's tux and the Judge in his magisterial robes as he performed the ceremony. Harry still wore a silk tie that he hadn't loosened.

As he continued his efforts to melt her bones, she slipped a hand up onto his chest and loosened that tie. Then he slid his hand down her back and onto her butt and grabbed on hard, pulling her tight against his thigh. The jolt that convulsed through her had her hand fisting around the Windsor knot.

One of them moaned. She was fairly sure that it was him, but she could feel it echo into her chest and down her body in ways that were going to lead to places she didn't want to go.

She pushed back against his chest. He protested, hung on tighter when she persisted, but finally gave in and let her ease back. Her head was spinning and deep gulps of cool salt air did nothing to clear it. Unable to release her fist, she pulled on the tie; the silk tail slid free as a smooth caress against her palm.

"Careful," Harry's voice was rough.

*Careful?* Who was he kidding? Careful didn't begin to cover the present dilemma. She started to take one more step—

Harry grabbed her wrist and tugged her sharply toward him. "Cliff," he croaked out before she could protest. A glance over her shoulder revealed that she was a single step from a hundred-foot tumble down to the beach.

"Uh, thanks." This time she was careful to sidestep but couldn't seem to slow her need to retreat from Harry Slater.

"Becky?"

"That's…" she searched for something to say. Something light, even funny. "That's a hell of a kiss you pack there, Counselor. You got a license for that thing?" It came out all whispery and dreamy.

"Nope," she could hear the smile in it even if it was too dark to see. He was regaining control of that smooth voice of his, so why couldn't she do the same with her own. "Unlicensed. Is the court going to fine me again?"

Not if the judge wanted to keep her sanity. "The, uh, court rests at this time. It will reconvene…" when more than two brain cells were firing with something other than the temptation to jump Harry Slater's bones here and now, "…tomorrow." At the very earliest.

She turned abruptly for the house and started to toward it. Even with the low heels of her dressy cowboy boots, she tacked across the lawn in a staggering line. The house practically throbbed with the sounds of the party that had all moved indoors by now: laughter, shouts, conversations, and a stereo pouring out AC/DC's *Back in Black*. With the assistance of the handrail she navigated the half dozen pitching steps up onto the verandah.

"Nice tie," a voice whispered from the shadows. Tiffany Mills sat on one of the porch swings. Her long hair had slid forward mostly hiding her face. It fell almost to her lap. She was knitting by the light spilling out from the living room window.

Becky looked down at her own hands. She still clutched Harry's necktie in a bunched fist. It was green with gold strips. Inside the narrow gold stripes she could see "Oregon Ducks" imprinted in a pale green. What was it with University of Oregon grads that they were such rabid fans of the Ducks even after a decade in New Orleans?

She dropped down to sit beside Tiffany and clutched the tie in her lap. "Thanks, I guess."

"Trophy?"

"I—" she'd never taken a boy trophy in her life. "I don't think so. I just couldn't seem to let go of it at the time."

"I might have noticed."

Becky glanced up. The horizon was invisible in the darkness. Then the lighthouse beam swept across the water. In the foreground, low bushes and the handrail for the beach stairs stood out as dark silhouettes. She and Harry would have been visible front and center in the vista. She watched carefully through a handful of sweeps of the light, but he was no longer anywhere to be seen.

Tiffany had returned to her knitting. Her actions at least made sense for the evening. Several years back Tiffany had purchased and cleared property up the hill, a mile past the lighthouse. She came down to town only for the Tuesday and Friday afternoon knitting sessions at the Lamont B&B and to sell her farm's excess produce. As far as Becky knew, this was the first time Tiffany had come to an Eagle Cove party of any sort. So it made sense that she would be sitting out here, away from the crowds, and enjoying being near rather than a part of the action.

Becky wasn't making any sense to herself at all. She was normally in the heart of any crowd and this was exactly her sort, local. There wasn't a person at the party she didn't know. It was fun and loud.

She barely managed to return a wave from Peggy as the Judge escorted her down the steps and away beneath the twinkle lights to where the cars were parked. Judge Slater was always the perfect gentleman, which was more than Becky could say for his son. She could still feel the warm palm print where Harry had grabbed her butt.

Instead of jumping up to rejoin the party, she was sitting out here in the cool darkness clutching a man's tie like a lifeline.

*What the hell?*

# # #

Which was exactly the same question Harry Slater was asking himself as he stared through the trees from his old bedroom window toward the shining lights of the Lamont's Victorian B&B.

He should be over there. If not picking up a bit of fun for the night, then at least catching up on some drinking with his old pals.

The big Douglas firs and a small copse of alder that rose between the properties were outlined by a thousand pinpricks of light from Jessica's party. It was a familiar sight. Gina Lamont, Jessica's aunt, was known for turning everything into an occasion. Sure, the bed and breakfast served up a fine and generous breakfast—he and Greg had slipped through the trees to avail themselves of leftovers any number of times. But guests were often in during the evenings as well. Rum cake, brandy, and boisterous euchre tournaments. Homemade chocolate chip cookies the size of a person's head and a murder mystery game that used the entire B&B grounds and every guest. He'd played the clumsy young sidekick to Gina's suave-and-sexy redheaded inspector any number of times back in high school.

He'd kissed Jessica for the first time on the widow's walk. A tiny space high on the roof of the B&B. Visible to no one, but open to the sky. He'd always thought his first kiss would be something stolen in a dark, cramped, and hurried way. Instead it had been an amazing exploration. Okay, an amazingly clumsy one, on both of their parts, but nothing like he'd ever imagined. And then Greg had impossibly popped up to completely ruin the moment.

He reached up to loosen his tie, and grabbed nothing but air. Where had it gone? He didn't remember taking it off earli—

Becky. He'd lost it somewhere while kissing Becky Billings. Well, no wonder he couldn't recall misplacing it. That kiss had seared everything else right out of his brain. She'd been apparently unaffected. Instead she'd stood at the cliff's brink—hip cocked and her broad smile shining in the darkness—*"You got a license for that kiss, Counselor?"*

No, but he was definitely going to find out where to register.

Harry dropped down onto his bed to stare up at the darkened ceiling. His room had been preserved like some crazy shrine. Plastic trophies were still scattered over the shelves. Photos of the Pufflings soccer team at regionals, crowded close together in their white-and-black uniforms. Their noses were all grease-painted like bright orange Puffin beaks—the fact that the beaks of the seabirds who roosted out on the big sea stack turned orange only during mating season was merely added motivation for a group of high school soccer players.

There was also the college memorabilia layered on through four years of visits home. School books from University of Oregon, even his third-string Ducks shirt—which had been for track-and-field as they didn't have a men's soccer team. Maybe it was just as well. He'd dated a wing-back on the women's soccer team for a while and, watching her play, he'd discovered just how small-town the Pufflings really were. He'd thought himself and Cal as fine athletes, which they'd been in the world of small-coastal-town sports. But that was a whole different scenario than the Pac-12 Ducks. Being a wing-back, Chrysse did have incredible stamina, which Harry had appreciated even if he could barely keep up with her.

Maybe he should look her up. He still wasn't sure what had happened there. They'd been hot and heavy for the last two years of school then he'd gone into law and she'd just…gone. Her parents were local, weren't they? Portland maybe? Wow! There was a dead brain cell.

His whole identity (and ego, he ruefully admitted) in Eagle Cove had been athletics…until he barely qualified for the Ducks' track-and-field team. And his top grades, only bested by Jessica Baxter, had been in a class of merely thirty-four students. Freshman year at U of O had been another harsh shock. It had taken six years of hard work to fix that. He'd graduated number two in his law class, but it had been a long hard climb to get there.

"Shit!" He was getting all morose. He went to shove himself out of bed. Anything would be better than lying here and being stupid about the past. Instead, he closed his eyes and drifted toward sleep.

It wasn't the six-foot of chocolate-skinned wing-back who came to mind.

Nor was it the five-ten of a brilliantly blond and ever-so-happy Jessica Baxter.

He fell asleep only aware of the imprint that the short but bountiful Becky Billings had left on his chest.

# Chapter 2

*B**ecky had risen at* five a.m. and watched the sunrise as she drove across the Coast Range—the long line of three to four thousand foot hills that separated the Oregon Coast from the Willamette Valley. The fog had been gentle, only dusting the hollows as she climbed and descended through Maxine Pass and on into one of the richest farming regions anywhere. Mostly thirty miles wide and running a hundred and fifty miles from north to south, everything grew in The Valley—as coasties referred to it.

But what she cared most about was the hops and this was one of the premier hop growing areas anywhere. Becky doggedly had cultivated her own special suppliers.

The sun was now clear of the high Cascade Mountains that climbed to the east of The Valley and was already warming the fields. As she wound her way along ever-narrowing roads, she rolled down the windows to her van. It was painted as dark brown as a stout beer, with "Becky Billings BlueBird Brewery" and "The 5B" in gold lettering as light as a cream ale. It was actually one of her prized possessions, the first thing she'd ever bought with her beer money. And she'd paid cash.

Her dad had left her the farm, one of the only ones squeezed into Eagle Cove, before he and Mom had gone snowbirding off. Unlike most snowbirds who went south to Tucson or Cabo during the long, damp-and-chilly months of a coastal winter, they'd gone north to Alaska. He was always sending her funny postcards: a cluster of a dozen or more polar bears and his note on the back, "Miss my cattle, taking up herding PBs. No nastier than Mr. Wooster." Mr. Wooster had been the orneriest bull anywhere in Coast County and it often cheered Becky to know he was now safely up in Tillamook a couple of counties to the north.

She'd sold Mr. Wooster and most of the dairy cattle to a farm close by the Tillamook cheese factory, and used that money for her first tanks and full set of gear. During the lean startup years she'd sold the farmhouse as well, and built herself an apartment in the barn loft. She spent most of her time there anyway to be close to her brewery.

With the addition of several new fermenting tanks, she could keep five types of beer in process at any time. This was only her third season experimenting with atypical flavors and this year she wanted to really break out into something interesting.

Cherry had to be rejected because once she'd had a Walking Man Black Cherry Stout from up in the Columbia Gorge and she knew there would be no matching it.

She briefly wished she had access to some of the tropicals, but local and fresh was a key element of her plans for The 5B; so no mango porter or papaya lager for her. Not that she lacked for ideas…September was always a problem for her. She wanted to do everything. The tail end of the blueberry season was hanging on, a nice sweetener for an ale. Cantaloupe was also beckoning to her as she drove past fields with massive wooden crates being filled with melons by migrant workers. A melon malt. Strawberries were long gone but late peach and nectarine were still around.

She'd start with Tovar Farm and then see what else she had to do. She'd warned them she'd be coming and was greeted by a wave from the back kitchen door as she pulled her van around.

"Good morning, Valeria," Becky called out as soon as she reached the door. "Alejandro please tell me you have some of your excellent coffee brewing." Valeria Tovar was Becky's height and just as full-figured. Alejandro was a lean whip of a man no taller than his wife with the first spots of gray in his dark black hair. They both had the dark skin, prominent cheekbones, and broadly open faces of their far south heritage of Oaxaca.

Alejandro rarely spoke to her but he served up the best coffee in the Willamette. At first she'd felt hurt by his silence, as if she somehow wasn't good enough or was too crass or maybe he thought women were a lesser lifeform. But one day Valeria had whispered that he was very shy around women. "Especially beautiful women like you." Becky knew better, but after that she always made a point of being extra nice to him.

Valeria offered a broad wink and let Becky in through the kitchen door—apparently she'd hit the right note in her cry for Alejandro's coffee. The ranch house looked like any normal triple-wide from the outside. A line of cherry, apple, and Willamette oak trees offered a wind and sun break to the west and south. To the east and north stretched several hundred acres of land that the Tovars had purchased and cultivated for twenty years now since they'd earned enough as migrant workers to stop.

Inside the manufactured home it was almost like stepping back into Mexico. The sun-yellow kitchen was accented with warm reds of thick clay cookware, hanging spices scented the air almost as thickly as the dash of chili in the brewing coffee, and a big table filled the middle of the room. Three bleary-eyed teens were shifting focus between plates of food and checking their packs for school.

Alejandro set stoneware mug of aromatic coffee in front of Becky as she sat. Valeria followed it moments later with a plate of *huevos rancheros*. She'd given up protesting years ago. When you entered Valeria's kitchen, you were fed. Tortillas and eggs, both fresh this morning. Alejandro's black beans, salsa from just-picked tomatoes…

"I'm moving in," Becky said as she always did. The flavors exploded in her mouth: rich, strong, powerful. Just like—

Becky nearly choked as she tried to reconcile dreamy thoughts with sharp salsa.

Just like Harry Slater's kiss. She'd expected the memories of that kiss to keep her awake all night trying to figure out what they meant. Instead she'd been sent straight to sleep with a happy smile. This morning it had been easy to discount it as "a moment at a wedding." At least she hadn't slept with him. But the powerful flavors had brought back that kiss with a body slam.

It exploded out of her more as a gasp than a choke. Unable to help herself, she turned to look over her shoulder back toward Eagle Cove. What was Harry Slater doing right now? And would he still be there when she returned?

"Who is he?" Valeria patted her on the back and thumped a glass of water down on the table which Becky took several quick sips of before regaining control of her breathing. Alejandro was eyeing her curiously.

"Who is who? All I did was choke on a chili." She went for her best innocent look.

Mara rolled her eyes. When a half-awake fifteen-year old girl rolls her eyes at you it couldn't be good.

Becky shrugged, "An old friend, back in town for a visit." Except that wasn't quite right. They'd never been particularly close during high school. He was a jock and she'd organized dances and the talent show. She'd even managed to put together a half decent production of *The Sound of Music* senior year, using the school gym for a stage. She'd tried to cast Jessica as Maria because she looked most like Julie Andrews, but was shouted down because Becky had the best singing voice in the class. Instead Jessica had played the baroness and she'd conned Cal Mason Jr. into the Captain's role. He wasn't a great singer, but he'd looked great onstage. He also hadn't been the least bit shy about practicing for the big kiss scene either.

But she'd never thought of Harry Slater much one way or the other. Too arrogant for her taste, which had only made him a likely target when she needed someone to pith. The Harry Slater *she* knew…

Except he wasn't. That much had been clear last night. First he'd stared at her breasts, which—to be fair—had been part of the purpose of the little black dress. But he'd recovered well, looked her in the eyes after that. She'd caught him staring at her from across the kitchen. There'd been a very satisfying heat in his eyes that had cheered her at first. But when he hadn't followed, too damn sure of himself had been her conclusion. Right up to the moment she'd slid into his arms on a whim.

An arrogant man would have groped, grabbed, or at least gone for the kiss. Instead he had held her and they had danced. Even a night's sleep and sixty miles away, it had her sighing. He'd been so…

Mara was watching her with a big smile on her face.

"What?" Becky asked.

"I know that look."

Valeria's big wooden spoon whacked down abruptly on Mara's plate startling them both.

"*Oye!*" She aimed the spoon at her daughter's nose. "My fifteen-year-old daughter, she does *not* recognize that look. *Comprendes?*" Then Valeria sighed and lowered her spoon, "At least not in your mother's hearing, *por favor. Si?*"

"*Si*, Mama," Mara only looked a little abashed.

Then the spoon swung around and centered on Becky's nose, "But I too know that look."

"Well, I don't!" Becky glared at the massive spoon hovering inches from her nose. She was not having that look about Harry Slater.

Mara skipped offering another eye roll and went straight to smirk as she shouldered her school bag. Her brother and sister did the same, thankfully without eye contact. Those two dutifully kissed their mother and father on the cheek before rushing out the door to catch the bus. The distant throb of its diesel engine was clear over the quiet fields. Mara stopped by Becky's chair and gave her a hug that took Becky by surprise, she barely had a moment to return it.

"I so know that look," Mara whispered in her ear. "That's a really good look," and then she was gone.

Becky tried to catch her breath as Valerie and Alejandro joined her at the table with plates of their own.

"She's amazing."

"*Si!*" Valerie agreed. "She's just like I was at that age and that is to be the death of me."

"I was already in love with you by that age," Alejandro whispered softly.

The look that the two of them shared took Becky's breath away.

That was what she wanted. She wanted a man to look at her like she was the most important thing in his life, just as he would be the most important thing in hers.

And that certainly wasn't going to happen with Mr. Harry Slater of Eagle Cove and New Orleans.

She turned to her breakfast and to the business at hand. "I need a half ton of your malted barley, of course. But I'm really hoping for some Mt. Hood hops. Please, Alejandro, tell me you grew some this season. And maybe a few hundred pounds each of Super Galena and Perle. Why is everyone growing Fuggle this year?"

Of course just because Harry wasn't a happy-ever-after sort of guy didn't mean she couldn't have some fun while he was still in town. If he was still in town.

# # #

Harry strolled along LBB Way, headed for The Puffin Diner. It lay in the heart of town. Which was something of an overstatement as the Eagle Cove business district was just five blocks long. The whole town was caught between the beach, the broad bay fed by the Eagle River, and the Coast Range forest.

LBB Way was the longest road in town. The woman who had platted the seaside part of the town had used all landside bird names and Little Brown Bird Way had been her nod to the myriad species that she didn't have enough streets to honor. It was almost two miles from the lighthouse and the two Victorian manor houses to the town. The lane snaked along the shore connecting houses and beach along the way.

He'd headed for his car this morning and then noticed that Dad's and Greg's were still parked at the house even though he knew they'd both be down at the diner. It was a fine clear morning, so he grabbed a light jacket and walked into town instead.

New Orleans was a walking city—in the tourist sectors only. You actually needed a psychiatric checkup if you were crazy enough to try and drive through the crowds in the French Quarter.

A lot of the locals walked most places as well, but that had never worked well for him. His firm's offices were in the downtown core and within a mile of every major courthouse, making all of them an easy walk under normal conditions.

The problem was, that his Oregon Coast blood had never thinned out to Gulf Coast weather—the Big Easy was thirty degrees hotter and far more humid. A half-mile walk could leave a man in need of a half gallon of Gatorade. Worse, it *would* leave him soaked through an eight hundred dollar suit. He exchanged Christmas cards with his Gravier Street dry cleaners; Eagle Cove barely had a dry cleaners (a pickup-and-deliver service that Trey ran out of his basement along with a towing and taxi service, if the old man hadn't died or his beater tow truck hadn't dissolved into a pile of rust yet).

Walking was how people got around Eagle Cove when it wasn't raining.

There were fewer For Sale signs along LBB Way than he remembered from his last visit three years ago—it had taken his mother's funeral and now his brother's wedding to drag him back to this town.

Jessica's mother, the town's real estate agent, must be busy. There was a new life to the town that showed itself in little ways. Emil's yard had been cleansed of the car he'd never gotten around to restoring as well as the stacks of salvaged building supplies that were never going to be used for anything. He'd actually mowed it for a change. Mabel's sign advertising fresh eggs had received a new coat of paint and a fifty-cent per dozen bump in price. The Sleepy Owl Hotel had several cars in the lot despite it being a September weekday.

Greg had said something about his wife being hired as the town's new marketing manager. Seemed an odd choice for a Chicago journalist who had wanted out of this town as badly as he had. Maybe it had just been an excuse for Jessica and him to move in with Dad.

Though it wasn't like they were cramping Dad's style. The Judge lived all alone in the big Victorian that had belonged to the town's founding family. The Lamont's place had belonged to their daughter and, if town history was to be believed, never a civil word traveled between the two houses.

Ma had passed three years before and Greg had taken up residence in the guest house, a charmingly compact copy of the main house. Now Jessica was living there with him, but apparently they had dinner most nights with the Judge. Better them than him.

Harry tried to imagine a more excruciating choice, but had trouble coming up with one. Despite being most of the way to retired, the Judge still ran his household the same way he'd run his courtroom, with absolute and iron control. Never a misplaced word was spoken, never a statement was made without carefully considered content, and never, ever was a voice raised—not in anger and not in joy.

Harry kicked a stone out of the road and then cursed as his toe throbbed. Instead of sneakers he should be wearing shit-kicker boots like Becky had last night. The ones…

No! She'd already cost him a night's sleep. He was not going to waste any more time thinking about her.

It was a cool morning. The sun always took a while to make its appearance over the Coast Range, not striking Eagle Cove for an hour or more after it had lit the sky. The beach below the bluff would be in shadow for another couple hours after that. As the road dipped down he could see a few tourists huddled about in their shorts and sweatshirts wondering why they'd ventured to the shore. The few locals up at this hour for their morning constitutionals were dressed in jeans, warm coats, hats, and gloves. Harry's light jacket wasn't up to the morning beach chill, so he stayed with the road as it climbed back up toward town.

He turned onto Beach Way. Flamingo Apparel was having a tiny tots display, backed by Eagle Cove t-shirts. He hadn't seen those before. It was a good design. He might even get one himself before he went back home. He went over for a closer look, which was safe because they weren't open yet. It was… one of Ma's eagles. Mom (a.k.a. Ma Slater) sold her paintings all up and down the coast and somebody had co-opted one of her distinctive eagles right here in her hometown.

His blood pressure was rising. How could someone steal her work? Goddamn, but he was going to sue somebody over…

In a corner of the window display hung a small lithograph of the same eagle. A sign advertised "Ma Slater reprints available for purchase in Grosbeak Gallery." Okay, maybe he wouldn't sue anybody. Reprints? That was smart. Continued use of copyright. He should have known that the Judge wouldn't miss a trick. It struck Harry as a damned bloodthirsty act, turning a buck by degrading Mom's work.

This end of town was still awfully quiet. He checked his watch, six-thirty. Too early for a decent body to be awake, except his was on Central Time. By eight-thirty he was typically well into his workday, unless there was a hot case on and he'd probably been there right through the night.

Merganser Weavings actually had a couple of tourists sniffing around. Danny McCall's wife had a gimp leg from a teenage boating accident and Danny had set her up with a shop in the front room of their house. She spent most of her time at a big loom close by the window. On warm days, she would slide the window wide and was practically weaving out on the porch. She always had time to chat, but not this morning.

Then Harry blinked, the name had been changed: Merganser Tours and Weavings.

Tours? In Eagle Cove? Taped to the glass were a couple of nice aerial shots of Danny's and Ralph Lamont's fishing boats. Bright banners declared: "Whale-spotting in Season!" "Deep Sea Fishing!" There was even a "Scenic Plane Flights" poster that showed a Stearman 4 soaring above the coast. Peggy Naron must have finally finished restoring that old biplane.

Something was going on in this town and it was disorienting. Nothing ever happened in Eagle Cove.

Cal would give him the lowdown. And maybe he'd find a way to ask about Becky Billings, except Cal's Blackbird Bakery had a line out the door. In September. *What the hell?*

The town was...busy. Half of the parking spots along Beach Way were taken despite the early hour. Next thing you knew they would put in parking meters.

The Flicker's marquee, at least the part not blocked by the massive chainsaw art flicker woodpecker clinging there, declared a "Northwest Local Film—*Overboard*." He'd barely been born when Goldie Hawn and Kurt Russell had done the filming just up the coast in Newport, but he knew the Newporters talked about it still. They really needed to get a life. Of course locals up there also talked about the filming of *Sometimes a Great Notion* along the Siletz River from even a decade earlier and it was... the "Coming Soon" attraction.

God spare him from small towns.

The Puffin Diner commanded the far end of Eagle Cove, closest to the boat docks. It was the oldest building in town—or at least the oldest foundation. The original log cabin trading post had washed out to sea in the "Great Gale" of 1880. Its loss was still referred to in the present tense even if it had only been a solitary fur trader's hut at the time. However, when it had burned at the turn of the century, the city founders had fought back with a stone foundation made of large boulders and mortar. Early photos showed a third grand Victorian had once stood in the town, but heavy rot and a builder with no imagination leveled it shortly after the Great War and a two-story in the American-foursquare style now stood there.

The Puffin Diner's deep verandah was supported by well-spaced columns guarding the large front windows without darkening them excessively. It was painted white with black trim and had a bright orange door, just like its namesake. The Judge really did like his Puffins. It was almost as if…but Harry knew that the man had no sense of humor.

Quite why Harry was seeking out The Puffin Diner when he could have had a quiet breakfast at home eluded him. But he climbed the steps, swung open the front door, and stepped into chaos.

# # #

"I love your farm, Alejandro."

He had led her out into the hop fields. Most were harvested, but a few of the later-maturing varieties still stood. Becky was glad she'd gotten here before the final harvest and had a chance to walk the fields.

She liked remembering the smell of rich earth and blooming plants later when she brewed.

At either end of the rows were massive wooden poles leaning outward and driven deep into the soil. Wires anchored straight down from their high tops and into the soil. Between each pair of outward-slanting poles a high wire stretched down the length of the field with only occasional supporting verticals along the way. In between the poles, green hop vines climbed up vertical lines that dangled from the high wire.

There was a serenity among the graceful towering plants. All of her worries seemed miniscule in comparison. Every vine climbed, reaching for the sun with a slow, undeniable patience. Its tri-form palmate leaves twisted to catch every bit of light. The tight clusters of hop flowers, looking like small green pinecones the size of her thumb, grew in thick clusters.

"There is a peace here," he acknowledged after a while.

She closed her eyes and imagined her toes turning into roots to dig down into the soil for nourishment and water. She turned her face until the sun shone, green and bright through leaves and closed eyelids, as if she too could be energized by sunlight.

Alejandro let her have her moment.

It was almost as if she was slow dancing in the arms of…

She dragged herself back to reality long before she wanted to. "I need a flavor, Alejandro." *And a subject change for my thoughts.* "Something that tastes of fall. Others do cherry well and yet it feels too early for melon to be as rich and sweet as I'd want."

"Come," was all he said and led her deeper into the towering rows of the fields.

She felt at home here.

This is where she came to life: in the fields and also in her brewery. There was a serenity to working the process. Every little thing changed the beer. She scrubbed her steel and copper mercilessly because that gave her a known baseline—something in the process that never changed. Then she tuned and altered. Cooking the mash, changing the ratios, late addition of more wort; everything affected the final outcome. And her brewing notes had to be as meticulous as the tanks. She would spend hour upon hour studying what she had changed and how it had been expressed in the final product.

They emerged from the end of the long row of hops and Alejandro moved beneath a pear tree to pluck a fruit. No, beneath an Asian pear tree.

She too took one and bit into the round flesh. The light brown skin broke easily and it crunched like an apple. The smooth fruit was a kiss on the tongue, and yes she would let thoughts of Harry drift in with that luscious flavor: soft, sweet, melony. But it wasn't the punch of cantaloupe or the juice of watermelon. It had the warmth of honeydew and the slightly foreign cast of Crenshaw both backed by the hint of pear. Like home and wild lands combined.

"Oh, this," she couldn't help but moan. "This, Alejandro, is exactly what I've been missing in my life."

He handed her a fruit picker, the long wooden pole felt warm against her palms—worn smooth by a hundred thousand pickings. The small cloth collecting-bag and the broad claw-like fingers let her pluck the pears one at a time. He took up another pole.

As the morning warmed, the two of them harvested the very best off the tree until she had several bushels of the perfect fruit.

# # #

The Puffin Diner was in as much of an uproar as Harry had ever seen it. The dozen and a half tables were packed. Several people milled about, craning their necks looking for an open seat. Ten people were at the counter which only had six stools. Yet more of the weary-blue Formica tables were empty of food than sported plates. The hunter green-and-mauve linoleum, that had probably been out of style even before *Overboard* was filmed, sported a scattering of tourist beach bags, dropped napkins, and a shattered plate with a tall stack that had been discreetly shoved into a corner rather than being cleaned up.

He was a gifted courtroom lawyer, able to gauge the judge's, the jury's, and even the crowd's mood.

*This* was an unhappy crowd on the verge of tipping over into anger.

A hand reached and in moments Cal Mason Sr. had one of his meat cleaver-sized hands clamped around Harry's upper arm. "Don't stand there gawking, boy. Go be useful for a change." He practically launched Harry across the dining room with a sharp shove.

The Judge intercepted him near the swinging door and was guiding him toward the kitchen with a hand on Harry's back. He could count the number of times on less than ten fingers his father had touched him. His hugs didn't count. They were offered only at the moment before departure and consisted of a side-arm hug accompanied by an awkward fist thump on the back.

"Can you cook?"

Harry took one look at the big commercial griddle. On the black surface there were several sets of pancakes, eggs, bacon, hash browns…the last more burned than cooked. The roar of the big fans didn't quite move enough air to hide the smell. Maybe long ago he could have, but he'd lived in New Orleans for the last eight years. The food was so good there, from street carts to gourmet eateries, that Harry didn't even have butter or eggs in his kitchen for a morning-after treat. "Not a chance."

"Then you have front of house."

Harry turned to look out through the wide, stainless steel service window. Rather than a neat spinner with orderly tickets and a line of plates to be delivered, it had become the depository of dirty dishes as anxious customers strove to clear the tables.

His father threw an apron at him, "Put that on. Good luck."

"Where's Greg?"

"Having the first morning of his married life. Tomorrow, he's back here whether he's done honeymooning or not." The last came out as close to a growl as Harry had ever heard from his father. A judgment had been made and the sentence delivered. Once the Judge did that, nothing ever changed. *Tough luck, little brother.*

"But—" Harry had never done waiting staff jobs. He'd worked through high school mowing lawns. And been a tutor to make spending money in college and law school. "Cooking and restaurants was always Greg's thing, not mine."

"*When all good people shall ride to the aid of those we owe,*" the Judge decreed.

"I'm a lawyer. I only do that for a large retainer fee," but he strapped the apron around his waist.

The Judge almost smiled as he waved a spatula in Harry's direction and turned to salvage what he could from the grill.

Harry tried to place the phrase. Constitution? Declaration of Independence? The Magna Carta? Didn't the phrase start with "In times of war," or maybe "tribulation" was in there somewhere?

Taking a deep breath, he grabbed a battered gray plastic washtub, an order pad, and a stack of menus. The Judge stopped his progress long enough to hand him a pen so he could write down orders on the pad.

Right.

Harry swung through the doors and into the fray just as he identified the source of the quote. King Theoden of Rohan speaking to Gandalf in *The Lord of the Rings*. And if he remembered correctly, the line was quite different in meaning. "Why should we ride to the aid of those who did not come to ours? What do we owe to Gondor?"

It was too late for Harry to ask why him and what did he owe.

He went for the coffee maker first and started figuring out how to brew more.

# Chapter 3

*H*arry *more collapsed than* sat in the chair. It was almost noon. He knew the Judge always closed the doors to newcomers at ten. Eleven had gone by before either of them noticed. And it had taken another hour to take care of the last customers and send them on their way with a full belly and a smile.

His father slid two plates onto the table and settled his big frame into the chair across the table. A pair of the Swiss cheese-mushroom omelets, bacon, English muffin, and the inevitable hash browns. The Judge looked even more haggard than he felt.

Harry forced himself back to his feet. Rather than filling two mugs, he grabbed two of the last clean empties and brought the whole coffee pot back to the table. Just before he sat he remembered that the Judge liked cream and had to go all the way back into the kitchen's big walk-in to find some. The kitchen looked as shattered as the front of house. Eggshells had long since overflowed the trashcan and clustered all around its base, dripping onto the tile floor. Splatters of pancake batter were strewn across every surface. And the stack of burned product overflowed onto one of the prep tables.

He fetched the cream and carried the whole carton back out to the dining room.

They ate in silence for a long time. If he felt like this at thirty-two, what must the Judge feel like at sixty-four? Harry didn't like that thought. No more than he liked that no trace of pepper remained in his father's salt-white hair. Or the heavy lines on his face.

"Why didn't you get a substitute if you were going to let Greg sleep in?"

"Underestimated him."

He'd just married the beautiful Jessica Baxter: valedictorian, journalist, marketer, the #1 "get" of Harry's senior year at Puffin High. Everyone had underestimated his little brother, everyone except apparently Jessica.

"I ran the Puffin Diner myself for years. I would just call out the orders and the people would come and pick them up. I considered that today would be no different."

Harry waved toward the front door and then flinched. A tourist was peering in through the glass while his wife pointed to the hours posted on the door.

"Are you open?" The man shouted through the glass despite the "Closed" sign and the one beneath it that read "Monday to Friday, 6-10 a.m." The Judge didn't open on weekends because he notoriously didn't much like tourists.

"No!" Harry did his best to not make it a cry of horror, but the couple scurried away as if he'd been a shrieking demon. He turned back to his father, "They were lined up out the door. You never had a chance."

"Ever since he came home three years ago, Greg has taken care of the front of house. The income has risen four-fold, and that was before Jessica started her marketing campaigns to attract more tourism to the town. I never really appreciated all that he does now. I should have."

"Well *I* do. That was insane." And he was going to have to take his clothes out to Trey. The khakis might machine clean, though the ketchup and the grease stains were worrisome. But his Hugo Boss shirt was a wreck. Damn, it was one of his favorites. He'd worn it in case…in case he ran into Becky Billings. How sad was that?

"What happened here?" Peggy Naron's voice rose indignantly from the kitchen. She must have come in the back door which he hadn't thought to lock. In moments she was at their side glaring at them. She wasn't much taller standing than the Judge was sitting, but her glare was fierce enough to have both Harry and his father easing back away from her.

"We were a little bit…overwhelmed," the Judge stated.

"Utter goddamn catastrophe," was Harry's take on it.

"I'm just glad that Harry showed up when he did or I might have had some trouble."

Harry could only gawk at his father. If he could have, he'd have pinched himself, but the shock was too great. As kids, he and Greg had called their father JRB, for the Wild West's Judge Roy Bean—the self-proclaimed "Law West of the Pecos." The hanging judge wasn't exactly one to hand out praise. Harry wished there'd been a court reporter present so that he could review the transcript, but he was fairly sure that a compliment had just been perpetrated.

"What are you gawking at?" Peggy was five-six, had a shock of dark-red hair pulled back into a bushy ponytail, and her figure was the only small thing about her.

She owned the local airport and gave helicopter and plane rides. A hundred exploits had been attributed to her by the kids of the town and she'd never denied a one. The crazier they got, the more likely they seemed; it was just the sort of woman she was.

"Um," Harry looked at his father, but he was watching Peggy intently. "Nothing, ma'am." And that wasn't just Southern politeness; she was the type of woman you said ma'am to.

"And you?" She turned her laser-powered glare on the Judge. "You were in trouble and you didn't think to call me?"

*Why would his father call Peggy?* Old friends, he supposed. The two of them went back forever.

"Sorry, Peg. Wasn't even thinking by the time my boy arrived. But we got through it okay."

"So I see," her sarcasm lay almost as thickly about the room as the detritus of the last meals. There wasn't a single thing in order. "Well, let's get it cleaned up, boys."

Harry rested his forehead on the table and whimpered.

A sharp knock rattled the front door.

"We're closed!" He shouted without looking up.

Peggy smacked him on the back of the head, driving his nose sharply against the dirty Formica.

"Ow!"

He heard her walk over and snap open the lock. Harry turned to see Natalya standing in the doorway. Now that was a serious looking woman. He tried to remember why they hadn't hooked up in high school. Bethany Garber's blond hair and blue eyes came to mind. As deep as a mud puddle, but she'd fed his ego just fine and his hormonal whims just fine too. Besides, Natalya Lamont had been dangerous as a teen and looked even more so now. Still, the challenge could be—

"I'm headed back to Portland."

Figured. His luck was running true to form, all bad.

"Becky called and needs someone to drive her van back. I'm not going to bother the lovebirds, so you're my next pick, Harry. Which means I must be desperate."

"Next pick for what?" Was he really such a bad choice? How bad was his reputation?

Natalya just looked at him with those dark eyes of hers. Apparently plenty bad. A pity that he couldn't argue it being wholly undeserved.

"Right. Why does she need someone to drive her van back? Where is she?"

"She's at the hospital in Salem. Seems she busted her leg or something. I couldn't tell because it sounded as if they had her on some pretty good pain meds. Let's go," she shook her car keys at him. "I have a meeting in Portland in four hours and there's three hours of road plus delivering you to the hospital between here and there."

"Becky's hurt?" Harry was already in motion, trying not to imagine the worst. Pain meds. Big ones? Maybe she'd been in a car accident or... "What the hell is she doing in Salem?" He'd assumed that she was simply somewhere around town. He'd been planning to swing by the brewery after breakfast, just to see what she was up to out there.

He was half out the door before he recalled the disaster he was leaving behind.

He considered counting himself lucky and just making good his escape. But he didn't like the way that felt.

Harry turned back and started to speak, but got stuck somewhere between starting his sentence with "Dad" and "Judge" simultaneously.

" 'Bout time!" Peggy scoffed at him. "Now you can go."

Harry still hesitated. The restaurant was a real mess and his father looked…old. He wasn't ready for that. "I'll—" he didn't know what. Arnold Schwarzenegger had ruined the "I'll be back" line for all time.

"Don't worry," Peggy rested a hand on the Judge's shoulder. "I'll help him."

Harry nodded and rushed after Natalya. It was only as he was climbing in her slick little Mini Cooper that he wondered about that gesture. Judge Slater was not a man to be touched lightly, but he hadn't reacted at all.

# # #

Becky opened her eyes when someone poked her on the nose. "Hey, Natya! Sho nice to shee you." She could feel her voice slurring, but couldn't find the energy to be interested in fixing it.

She was still in the Emergency Room. Curtains turned her personal, private corner of it into an eerily dangerous place seen in too many television shows. But she wasn't hooked up to any of the machines which she'd take as a good sign. Well, except for the one giving her an IV drip of painkiller and she didn't mind that one at all.

Then her eyes focused on the man looking down at her over Natalya's shoulder. "Ooo! Pretty! You brought me a pretty!"

And Harry Slater was very pretty. He hadn't inherited much from the Judge, but like his father, Harry's face had more character than…Indiana Jones. If you took Harrison Ford, made him blond, changed the color of his eyes…he'd still look nothing like Harry. The man looked like…himself. She was really having trouble connecting thoughts.

"What did they put me on?"

"I don't know," Harry grinned down at her. "But by that smile, I want some."

"Sure. But then who would drive me home? You'd have to crawl into this hospital bed with me."

Harry's smile lit up in a way that made her giggle. Damn but he was cute; every thought moved so clearly across his features.

Natalya rolled her eyes, "I should have brought the Judge instead."

"No! You brought me a pretty. I wanna keep my pretty."

Natalya looked quickly at Harry and then back at her before narrowing her eyes. Then in one of her lightning quick mood changes, she smiled brightly and Becky almost forgot that momentary look of suspicion. "So, what did you do?"

"Hish fault," she pointed an accusing finger at Harry, careful to use the arm without the IV in it. "I stood up too soon as I stepped out the back door of my van. Shoulda ducked longer." Right. Her head. Reaching up, she found a bandage taped high on her forehead. Even through the drugs she could feel a sharp pain when she found the massive lump. "Then I fell, but snagged my boot on a crate of Asian pears. My knee made an awful noise. All crunchy."

Harry winced and paled.

"Like dropping a bag of pretzels on a concrete floor. Crunch! Crunch! Crunch!"

Harry went sheet white. Natalya knew exactly what she was doing and just offered her an evil smile that Harry wouldn't be able to see as he still stood behind Natalya.

"Valeria and Alejandro wanted to stay, but they have barley on the malting floor. I forced them to leave as soon as we found out it was just a really bad sprain and you said you'd bring the cavalry. Didn't know the cavalry was so pretty." Even to herself she was sounding fairly stupid, but the drugs just made her happy to go with the flow.

"How…" Harry swallowed hard and looked about the curtained corner of the E.R.

Becky checked. Still not hooked to any machines. Good.

"How is this my fault?"

"Thinking 'bout…" the drowsies were coming back, "…you. 'Stead of my head." Her eyes drifted closed though she fought against it. "Sh-cared poor Alejandro spitless."

# # #

Natalya's sudden grasp on Harry's arm was painful. She'd hit a nerve junction of some sort.

"Hey! Ow!" He tried to shake her off which only hurt more. In moments she'd dragged him out of the E.R. and into the parking lot. Salem was twenty degrees warmer than Eagle Cove and the sun felt bright and hard unlike the way it shone softly on the coast.

She pushed him up against the side of Becky's van before releasing him. She did it hard enough that he bunged his elbow right on the funny bone.

"Cut it out, Natalya!"

She poked a finger into the center of his chest, "Can I trust you?"

"What are you talking about?"

Natalya growled. It was a dangerous sound that didn't make him think of dog or cat; it was pure pissed-off woman.

"What am I missing?" It was one of his better skills that nothing took him by surprise. He could adjust faster than most lawyers and better than any witness to changing circumstances. But he had no insights in this situation.

"That," Natalya jabbed a finger toward the E.R., "is one of my very best friends. I don't know what you did to her last night. She was all strange after the reception and now I know whose fault that is. Don't even think about going there, Slater. She's drugged out and she's going to be hurting. You so much as blink wrong and I'll know. I'll come down from Portland and castrate you with a rusty butter knife."

"Christ, Natalya! What sort of a man do you take me for?"

She hesitated, then shifted back onto her heels, giving him a little breathing space. "I don't know you anymore, Harry. I've barely seen you since we both went to college. But I most certainly knew the shallow troll that was Harry Slater."

"Well," he wished that description hadn't once fit him so well, but there wasn't much point in arguing. "Even then I wasn't the sort who takes advantage of a woman under pain meds. You have my word as a member of the Bar Association on that one." He wasn't quite sure why he felt compelled to add that last. In New Orleans there'd been no past to live down. He'd simply arrived and made himself into the man he was today. If asked before the last two days, he'd have said he did a halfway decent job of it. But the women of Eagle Cove were definitely keeping him off balance.

"And you find Becky attractive?"

"Shit, yes!" And only after he answered did he catch her change in tone. He hadn't been ready for a friendly, casual question in the midst of a cross-examination. Hadn't meant to speak that truth to a woman threatening him with bodily harm. "Damn but you'd have made a good attorney, Natalya."

Natalya checked her watch and then cursed. "I'm going to be late. You take care of her, Harry. Can you do that for me?"

He raised three fingers in a Boy Scout salute, "Scout's honor." He'd been a lousy Boy Scout.

She rolled her eyes at him, because of course she knew that about him. Couldn't get away with crap in a small town. Then with another curse she checked her watch again, rushed over to her Mini Cooper, and cranked it to life. She backed out of her spot until the driver's side window was close beside where he still leaned against the van.

"Don't screw it up, Slater, or you're dog meat!" Then with a harsh chirp of her tires, she was racing out of the lot and back onto Mission Street.

Harry headed back into the E.R.

Becky was waiting for him in a wheelchair. They must have given her a wakeup med, because her eyes were bright. That too-bright of over-medication. He was used to seeing it from his days defending low-lifers back in criminal court. He'd escaped to civil court as fast as he could, at least corporate clients didn't try to knife you when you asked for your fee.

He didn't like the bandage on her forehead either. She wore a denim workshirt that still sported a couple dribbles of blood that some E.R. nurse had been kind enough to try and sponge off. Her right leg was wrapped in a brace and propped up on the wheelchair's raised leg support.

"Nice skirt," it was all he could think to say to cheer her up. He didn't like seeing Becky Billings looking sad as she fingered the top of the leg brace. And the skirt was nice; as different from last night's little black dress as you could get. Bright splashes of color: reds, blues, and golds, as if she'd pulled on a flower garden.

"Valeria's. The woman thinks of everything. Even as they were loading me into the ambulance, she knew I wouldn't be able to get back into my jeans." On cue a nurse handed him a bag. It contained a pair of battered work boots, socks, folded up jeans, and a set of bright blue panties covered in giant sunflowers. Which meant that under her skirt she was wearing—

Harry could feel his breath growing short as the nurse handed him a pair of crutches. Which worked as thoroughly as a cold shower.

The nurse rattled off a set of instructions about time off the leg, time on the crutches, follow-up appointments with the local doctor, and so on. He should be taking careful notes, and under normal conditions his mind was a steel trap for such information. But Becky: sad, battered, yet still sexy as hell in a wheelchair, was the ultimate distraction to his thoughts.

"Here," the nurse flapped a sheaf of papers as thick as a trial pleading under his nose. "This covers everything I've just said. Take these top two sheets to the pharmacy down the hall to get the prescriptions filled."

"Okay." In a daze he was wheeling Becky down the hall. The view wasn't all that different from his first look down at her in the kitchen last night. But instead of a jaunty attack on the world, her head was tilted sadly down. He raised a hand off one handle and stroked it down the long flow of golden brown.

"It'll be okay, Becky."

She nodded in a very unconvinced manner.

And then, because he'd only kept one hand on the handles, he practically rammed her into a wall.

When she didn't even tease him about his driving, he really began to worry.

# # #

Becky lay back in the passenger seat and tried not to scream at her leg. It was throbbing through the narcotic, which was making her stomach churn through the anti-nausea drug, which made her so...*angry* at the world.

She didn't have time to be hurt.

The van was filled with almost a ton of malted barley, dried hops, and Asian pears at their peak of ripeness. She couldn't afford to miss one day, never mind the ten that the nurse had told her to stay off her leg. Truly couldn't afford it. Part of being a supplier was that her clients, taverns and restaurants, expected a steady and reliable supply. If they ran out of 5B beer, they'd just roll someone else's keg into place and she'd have to fight like a demon to get the slot back by offering special price incentives that she could ill afford. She was being a success, but lately that was a seventy hour-a-week proposition with time off only for best friends' weddings.

And the Asian pears didn't have ten days either. They were picked at the moment of perfection and were now scenting the van with their soft, sweet tease. If they weren't in boiling copper within two days, she might as well throw the whole mess away.

"Talk to me, Harry. About anything. So far you've just driven in silence clutching the wheel like a concentrating drunk. Anabelle is a sweet girl and only needs a light hand."

"Anabelle?"

"Go ahead, tell me that your Beamer or Porsche doesn't have some testosterone laden name. Max from *Mad Max* or Luthor, from Superman's arch enemy."

"Clive, my Mercedes Roadster—"

"SLK or SL?"

"SLK. The 350," he said it cautiously. Harry looked over at her for the first time since they'd gotten her into the van and buckled into place. He hadn't taken even the tiniest bit of advantage as they'd brushed and bumped together while figuring out how to maneuver her from wheelchair to the front seat.

"Wimp!" For two reasons, but she wasn't going to mention the second one. Even if she hadn't been in the mood for flirting, it would have been nice if he'd at least tried.

"I'm a wimp for owning an SLK?"

"C'mon," she loved that her tease was working. "The SL has half again the horsepower."

"And twice the price tag."

"Wimp!" All that time she'd spent online daydreaming over a hot driving machine a few months back hadn't turned out to be a waste of time after all.

Harry drove for another mile down the freeway in silence before turning once again and sticking his tongue out at her.

"Bring that here and I'll kiss it for you."

"Not a chance, Billings." With that he returned his attention to the road.

*Not a chance?* Sure, kissing Becky Billings had been fun at a wedding reception, but not good enough for every day. Especially not for a man like Harry Slater. Double especially not now that she was broken.

Well, he wasn't going to see her crying over it.

She closed her eyes and let the rocking of the heavy-laden van combine with the narcotic fuzziness and nausea to transport her away from this moment. Away from the heat burning in her eyes. Way far away.

# # #

The sun was well to the west by the time Harry was creeping the van toward Becky's.

"Not the house," she murmured, her first words in a hundred miles. It had been lonely, but he was glad that she was sleeping. Must have had a hell of a day and sleep was probably the best thing for her.

The house was nothing much. Just a small two-bedroom place at one end of the fields. A truck and a minivan were parked close beside it. Somehow he'd had the impression that Becky lived alone.

"Had to sell it in the early years to get going."

Oh.

Past the house stood an old hip-roof red barn. Becky's family had kept forty head of cattle, mostly dairy and some beef. His family's freezer had often had half of a Billing's cow done up as steaks, roasts, and burger. There was nothing like grass-fed beef. He'd forgotten how much he missed that flavor.

But no longer. The fields were all deep in hay from the house out to the barn near the little airstrip. The hangar with Peggy's truck parked beside it stood only a hundred yards way.

"The barn?"

"Around the side," Becky's voice was rough, probably from just waking up.

The driveway led to a well-mowed and tended parking area capable of holding ten or more cars. The old calving barn had been spruced up. It was a single story extension off the side of the main barn perhaps thirty by forty feet. Cheery clumps of mums and *Rosa rugosa* grew to either side of a broad double door with diamond-shaped glass panes. The siding had been painted the same colors as Becky's van, dark brown with golden lettering: "Becky Billings BlueBird Brewery, The 5B's Tasting Room." He'd forgotten about her nickname of Bluebird.

"Do you still sing?" She'd had far and away the best voice in the school. Her Maria in *The Sound of Music* had been great. A little…actually a lot sexier and sassier than Julie Andrews, but it was Becky Billings after all.

"In the shower," she bit off the admission.

"Pity." And it was. He didn't know much about singing that he didn't pick up from the playlist on his phone. It wasn't as if she should have pulled up and gone to Nashville, but there'd always been merry humming or singing whenever Becky was around. "Your singing was always a really happy sound."

She looked at him strangely. Again his training failed him and he couldn't make any sense of it.

This whole side of the barn had been fixed up. She waved him toward a big cargo door for loading hay that stood close beside the converted tasting room. It had a person-sized door built in.

"Back in."

He eased the van into place, shut it down, and came around to help her. By the time he reached her she was a tangle of seatbelt, crutches, and frustration. He tugged the crutches from her hands and stood them against the side of the van. Then he unraveled the seatbelt.

She wouldn't look up at him. Embarrassed? Sorry to have been a burden? Or just because she was hurt?

Unable to stand the tightness in his chest from watching her, he leaned in and scooped her up into his arms.

"Hey!" Becky started to squirm.

"Don't do that, unless you *want* me to drop you?"

She went absolutely still for a moment and then relaxed enough that it felt as if he was carrying a woman and not a mannequin. Thankfully he'd kept her keys in his hand and was able to unlock the brewery door without having to set her down.

As they crossed the threshold, Becky reached out and flicked a light switch. Harry could only stop and gawk. The stalls had been ripped out and walls raised to create a sealed room. There were rows of gleaming steel tanks—some tall, others squat. A big copper kettle shaped like an upside-down wine glass from the bowl to halfway up the stem dominated the center of the room. Stainless steel piping connected tanks with big valve handles along the way. A control panel fit for an aircraft carrier stood off to one side.

"Holy shit, Billings!"

"Beautiful, isn't it?"

"Beautiful? No. Scary maybe," he made a show of peering about cautiously. "Any monster creation I should know about, Dr. Frankenstein?"

"Not a one." For the first time since they'd left the E.R. the tease was back in her voice which was a major relief. "Well, maybe one or two little ones, just, you know, knee-high maybe. I'm still starting out."

Harry gazed at the bewildering array of shining equipment. "If this is just starting out, I'm completely humbled."

"It's way easier than what you do."

"Law? That has got to be simpler."

"You don't need seven years of schooling to do this. You can put me down."

"Well sure, but they don't teach lawyers anything about alchemy and magic, especially not with such high-tech cauldrons." He wasn't ready to set her down yet. She was trim. And while that didn't make her weightless and his arms were tiring, he liked the feel of her curled against his chest.

"I do have a book of secret formulas."

"Can I see it? I promise not to understand a single thing. I'm merely curious about what real-world magical formulas look like."

"Maybe. Now put me down, Harry."

"Sure, where?"

She pointed toward a set of rough stairs that led up to the hayloft, "I have an apartment up there."

"You have a bum leg remember. That's not going to happen."

"I— Damn it, you're right. I hate that you're right."

"Me personally?" His arms really were aching. He spotted a battered couch that looked well lived in and set her down on the cushions.

"No, the fact that I can't even go home," she looked toward the stairs again and appeared about to cry.

He was certainly not ready for that.

Now he saw that the couch was part of a small living area set in the corner of the brewery. It had all of the basic amenities: couch, an equally well worn and cushy armchair, coffee table, a tiny two-burner kitchen area, and most importantly a bathroom. It was…he surveyed the area…it was for the nights when she had to pay attention to some critical stage of the brewing process. That meant that he'd set her down wrong.

He shifted some of the couch pillows and patted them. "Here," he supported half her weight as she moved to the other end of the couch, and ended up facing her vast array of brewing apparatus.

She was scowling up at him with a look of deep concentration. "What?"

"When did you become so observant?"

"Lawyer, remember. Part of the job description."

"And so thoughtful?"

"Oh, well that part of it is just a mistake. I won't let it happen again."

That finally earned him a Becky laugh. It was a short one, but he could detect none of the earlier bitterness in her tone.

He glanced at his watch, "Crap!" He rushed out to the van to retrieve her crutches and her drugs. She was past time for the next painkiller and the nurse and the pharmacist had warned him about not getting behind on the pain meds for the first couple days.

# # #

Becky let him pamper her, mostly because she didn't have a choice. Her emotions were in such chaos that she barely knew which way was up.

Harry had made it clear that he didn't want to kiss her again. Hadn't said a single thing during the whole drive while she fought back tears.

Then he carried her about as if she was a fairy princess rather than a broken garden gnome. And he'd admired her brewery. Not just, "That's nice," like most people, but he'd been seriously impressed.

What she really hadn't been ready for was the perception that somehow told him that she would always choose to face her brewery. Then he'd rushed back in from the van as if being twenty minutes behind on her meds was an international crisis. Actually the way her knee was feeling half an hour later, those twenty minutes were at least of statewide if not national concern.

"Perhaps I should call out the National Guard."

"Don't need them. You have me," Harry startled her as he came back into the brewery. He'd said that he would be right back after watching her take the meds, but then had driven away in her van and she had no idea why. Harry held aloft a brown paper bag. It smelled of…

"Oh my god!" She couldn't keep the squeak out of her voice.

"Yes!" Harry did a little dance step. "The man nails it!"

"Screw that! Gimme!"

And in moments he had a pair of May Conklin's burgers from the Brass Plover Pub and a massive load of onion rings spread out on the small coffee table. He perched down past her feet.

She grabbed the burger that he held out.

"I brought Cokes because you can't have alcohol with your meds."

She didn't point out that she had several hundred bottles of cider, root beer, and other 5B sodas sitting on the shelves not twenty feet away.

"What inspired you to such perfection?" She took a monstrous bite and closed her eyes to appreciate the good beef, Mr. Greene's garden-fresh tomatoes and lettuce, and May's trademark sauce.

"Because you don't have crap in your fridge," he waved a hand toward her kitchenette. "Don't forget. You're supposed to have food with your meds."

"My kitchen," she mumbled around another mouthful, "is upstairs and very well stocked. Not that I'm complaining."

Harry gazed up at the ceiling for a long moment as he chewed. "Right. Forgot about that. I'm not much of a cook anyway."

"You just haveta have the right kitchen."

And again with that fine perception of his, he glanced over his shoulder at the brewery rather than back at the ceiling.

"Come here."

He eyed her carefully as if trying to gauge her intentions.

As if she could be any more obvious. It was as if she'd misread him again, but she didn't think so.

Harry inspected his half-eaten burger but didn't take another bite.

"If it's not me—"

"It's not you," Harry cut her off.

"Then what?"

"Look," and she could see him trying to pull on his reasonable-lawyer cloak. "You're hurting and you're on Schedule II narcotics. If I took advantage of that, I'd be no better than… than dog meat."

"Dog meat? That's Natalya's favorite threat. She cornered you, didn't she?"

Becky could see it on his face.

"I love Natalya to death, but for this I just might have to kill her. Is that the reason you've been acting so strangely around me all day?"

"Her points on decent and proper behavior have a valid basis—"

"Counselor, shut up!"

It took him a moment, but he closed his mouth. Then a grin slowly formed. It didn't start at his lips, it started with those ocean blue eyes.

"The court has ruled. I am not Natalya's little sister despite my size. And being of sound mind and body, I hereby order you to kiss me."

"Well," the grin had reached his lips. "I can't speak to the mind, but that is some body you have."

"Stop quibbling."

And he did.

It wasn't a scorcher like last night, or maybe that was the buffering of the drugs, but Harry didn't leave much else to complain about. It was just lip to lip as they both still held their burgers, which made it only the second best kiss ever committed…anywhere, ever.

Her head was spinning long after he leaned back and resumed eating his burger with a cat-and-canary smile.

"Don't need any drugs as long as I have access to that," she muttered to herself.

"I have a supply in stock."

"Good, give me another dose."

"I'm busy eating."

She couldn't wipe the smile from her face as they continued their meal. Okay, she had a blown knee, a knot on her forehead the size of a quahog and a brace most of the way up to her crotch. But she did have a whole lot to smile about at the moment.

Then she looked up at her vats and tanks. The latest fermentations needed checking. And the mash tun and kettle were both empty—waiting for the ton of product stacked right now in the back of her van.

She decided to worry about all that in the morning.

She barely noticed when strong hands tucked a blanket around her.

The kiss on her forehead was a soft caress.

# Chapter 4

*The cell phone ringing* eased Harry awake with all of the grace of an electric chair. His nerves were jangling as he managed to answer it.

By a dim worklight in the brewery, he could see that Becky was still asleep on the couch. And his back could feel every second of sleep he'd managed while slumped in the armchair.

He didn't want to disturb her and hurried out the door before speaking. It was still dark and a chill bit at his bare arms.

"This had better be good," not his most gracious greeting. Especially not if it was one of the partners at Parrish, Merryfield, and Roland operating from another time zone. Harry was in the final year of the partner track—the one senior associate that everyone knew was a shoe-in. They rarely tapped more than one a year, but the firm's director had made it clear he was in, without making promises of course.

"Peggy has a flight this morning and Greg and Jessica left town," the Judge began without preamble.

"Why didn't you stop him?"

"I had told him to take the week off and I have never been one to go back on my word, despite my ill-spoken sentiment yesterday morning."

"And you're calling me because…" Please tell him he was wrong.

"Your assistance this morning would be appreciated. Am I correct in assuming that you're in town?" His father was careful not to ask where he actually might be as he hadn't come home last night. "Passed out drunk on Cal's couch" had been too likely a response to that question in his younger days. There was no point lying about anything in a small town, especially not in the Judge's house.

"Yes," he was in town though he wished he could have said no.

"Fine. We open in twenty-eight minutes."

And Harry was holding a disconnected phone. "I never agreed to help, you arrogant prick!"

Shouting at a cell phone in the middle of the night. Really useful; but it was more than he'd ever managed or would manage to his father's face. Twenty-eight minutes. Okay, it wasn't the middle of the night. It was five thirty-two in the morning. Because, if the Judge was anything, he was punctual.

There wasn't time to get home, shower, and change. Eagle Cove wasn't big, but LBB Way wasn't exactly a raceway and Becky's was on the far end of town.

He tiptoed back into the barn-turned-brewery.

Upstairs he discovered that a section of the hayloft had been walled off. It was a single space that was both cozy and rustic. Windows to one side opened onto darkness, and to the other they revealed the unfinished section of the hayloft, still partly stocked with large bales of sweet grass.

Becky had wrestled a king size bed up the stairs, it was covered with a quilt made from all the colors of the sea. It started dark in one corner and went through a storm-tossed transition of intricate piecework before finally emerging in the lighter tones. A good kitchen made of salvaged materials dominated the other end of the room: a large cast iron sink, refinished planking thick enough to park a tractor on, and odd-sized cupboards that looked more appropriate for animal tack than human food.

In a corner stood a toilet and clawfoot tub. What was it that women had against showers? The clawfoot had a curtain on circular rod, but the spray nozzle was a handheld on a steel flex-hose coiled about the faucets.

All open plan. Becky either never entertained up here or she had no modesty around her partners. He very much liked the image of a naked Becky cooking in the kitchen in easy view from the bed. He didn't like the image of Becky here with another man. Possessiveness wasn't really his thing, but he didn't like it anyway.

Something was missing and it took him a moment to figure out what. The loft apartment had no living room. No desk. Becky might sleep, cook, and bathe up here, but she lived downstairs close by her brewery.

He shed his clothes, trying to ignore the intimate sensations of being naked in her bedroom, and washed himself quickly. Just like the plumbing in the brewery downstairs, it was perfect—hot and plentiful.

There was nothing else to change into other than yesterday's clothes. They felt clammy and grimy. They were still stained with grease and ketchup from yesterday's diner disaster.

"And today is looking so much better." Maybe instead of dry cleaning he'd just have them burned. He found a toothbrush still in its packaging and used that.

He left a note and things she'd need where Becky couldn't help but see it and kissed her lightly on the forehead. Unshowered, injured, and hurting, she was about the damn cutest thing he'd ever seen all tucked under her blanket with little more than her hair showing.

He resisted, just as he had last night, his urge to do so much more. Natalya had been right to trust him, even if she didn't. But he could at least wish he was a little less honorable.

# # #

Becky woke to the start of her van's engine. It was dark except for the nightlight she kept on in the brewery—she'd banged her shin more than once when some overpressure alarm had gone off in the early days or a timer had run out. Now her living room was never truly dark.

It was so quiet that she could hear the gear shift lever dropping into place and the parking brake clunk off.

Someone was taking her van.

She heaved the blanket aside, swung her legs off the couch—

And landed in a heap on the floor between the couch and the coffee table on which she banged her elbow.

Her knee. A leg brace. And as she lay on the floor, a slow cascade of pills rolled off the edge of the table and began piling up inches from her nose.

Pain meds.

She'd blown out her knee, which used that moment of awareness to start hurting like mad.

But that still didn't explain her van.

She sat up as well as she could to stem the flow of pills. The concrete was damn cold through her thin skirt. Valeria's skirt.

A quick sniff of the air told her that the brewery was okay. No scent of overcooked mash or a fermenting tank having outgassed yeasty air through an overpressure valve. No scent of warm copper from a working kettle either. In fact, the kettle was cold because…all of the product that was in the back of her van was currently crunching down the gravel drive and off into the distance.

As she gathered pills, she spotted the note.

> *Gone to help Judge with breakfast.*
> *Rest easy. Take meds with food.*
> *I'll bring back lunch.*
> *H.D.S.*

H.D.S.? Oh, Harold Davis Slater. Or was it Harold David? She didn't even know.

He'd left a container of yogurt, a banana, and an energy bar on the table for her which was awfully sweet. The last time a man had made a meal for her had been her father making waffles the morning before climbing into the RV and heading north. It wasn't much of a meal, but Becky wasn't going to tell Harry how many bonus points it had earned him.

She opened the yogurt, but there was no spoon. And her crutches were…she scanned around…leaning by the door a good dozen steps away.

"Missed that one, didn't you, Harry?"

Becky leveraged her cold butt back onto the warm sofa. From there she achieved her feet and immediately wished she hadn't. The brace didn't compensate nearly enough for putting weight on her bad leg. Raising it so that she could hop across the room wasn't much better; she more ran into the rough barn wall than reached it.

She added splinters to her list of woes. Harry was rapidly losing those bonus points. With her crutches she made it to the bathroom, fetched a spoon and a juice in the kitchenette, and hobbled back to the couch. Breakfast and taking her meds lasted about two minutes.

She checked her phone, rather she tried to. It wasn't anywhere to be found. She could almost picture it…on the dash of the van. Crap! The big clock above the brewery's control panel read six a.m. Harry would be back in about five hours. What in the world was she supposed to think about for five hours?

Certainly not Harry Slater.

Her other option was staring her in the face. She could think about all of that gleaming hardware standing there doing nothing.

She'd be better off thinking about Harry.

# # #

Harry decided that he'd be better off dead.

He had the coffee maker figured out, so that part of it was okay. And to replace the soiled Hugo Boss the Judge had found him an Eagle Cove t-shirt with more of Ma's art on it. He only wore t-shirts when he played racquetball and it left him feeling strangely exposed. Ma's art made him feel like a walking billboard for opportunistic exploitation. Didn't the man respect anything about his wife's legacy? Every local would recognize it and know that her son was wearing…

Least of his problems.

It took him a while to understand that the Judge had very specific rules of the kitchen, which really shouldn't have been a surprise, but it was.

He offered omelets five different ways that weren't written down on the menu; thankfully the locals knew them and Harry soon had those down. Pancakes came in two different-sized stacks. And oatmeal apparently only ever existed in one, single form: with sliced dried apricots and diced apples. Everything came with a side of farm sausage and hash browns—neither was optional. Marshmallows in hot chocolate were also considered a punishable crime for anyone tall enough to rest their elbows on the table without a high chair.

Harry ignored him on the last point because the other option was whipped cream from a can. When he found the stash of several bags of tiny marshmallows hidden in the server's station he decided that just maybe Greg was an okay little brother, even if he did marry Jessica Baxter and then skip town just because it was his honeymoon.

The problem was that the Judge's omelets were absolutely incredible and everyone in town knew it.

That meant the tables filled rapidly and stayed that way. Every time he looked out the big front windows, he saw another person walking toward their end of town along Beach Way. It was like a zombie apocalypse or something; they just kept on coming.

Because they stayed mostly full, there were seventeen wrong tables that he could deliver an order to, using the process of elimination. His average hit rate of the correct table was awful. He finally started marking the tickets with quadrants of the room: north, east, south, west.

"Greg has the tables numbered," the Judge kept offering him service tips across the pass-through window. This time it was accompanied by three omelets and a tall stack that went to one of the five tables of four people each in the west corner by the door, but he had no idea which one. Or did it go to the two sets of two. If the Judge offered more variety, it would be easier… but he didn't…so it wasn't.

"How are they numbered?" He had already proven that a tray was a bad idea in his hands, so he grabbed the first two plates, then cursed. It was about the hundredth time this morning that he'd forgotten to use hot pads. The Judge served his plates very well warmed. His father's hands might have calluses of iron, but Harry's didn't.

"No idea," the Judge actually looked chagrined. "He just makes it work."

"Thanks for the helpful tip." He grabbed the two plates again using hot pads and went in search of their owners.

# # #

Becky spent the morning going quietly insane.

Thoughts of Harry distracted a woman only so long when she had nothing more than a pair of nice kisses and a slow dance to base them on.

Her reading material was upstairs, as was her laptop. She eyed the climb several times, but her antics of the morning were still having repercussions. There was a demon poking at the inside of her knee with a sharp knife, and every time she stood up the room gave a nasty spin that sent her plummeting back to the cushions.

If she was her old self, dressed in jeans, she'd just scoot up the stairs on her butt. However, ruining Valeria's beautiful skirt was not an option and the inevitable splinters that would jab through the thin material and into her behind didn't sound like much fun either. The tasting room didn't have hours today, so she didn't need to worry about that.

If she had her goddamn phone, she could call Peggy for help. But her phone was…where? Oh, parked down at The Puffin Diner. Maybe if she wrote a note to herself she'd remember that for more than fifteen minutes.

Harry's score had slipped below par and was rapidly sliding down the cliff and being washed out to sea.

For lack of anything else to do, she managed to fetch her recipe books. They were her prized possessions and she kept them locked in a small fire safe she purchased for just that purpose. So far there were four thick, leather-bound journals in the series. She had to make three trips to get back to the couch. Why four books hadn't taken two or four painful, weaving trips rather than three was something she couldn't figure out at the moment.

Each one had been horridly expensive, especially in the beginning. Custom hand-tooled leather outside and handmade paper within. Barry did such beautiful work and she'd forked over the cash for each one because she wanted her business to be a real and serious business. No fooling around, no cutting corners. One hundred percent the best the whole way. She brushed her fingers over the hand tooling, "5B" with roman numeral volume numbers worked into the soft leather. She loved holding the journals. These were her children, for now. At least until she found the right man.

There was a laugh. If Harry Slater was anything, he wasn't the right man. Worldly, handsome, living the high life in New Orleans with his Mercedes-Benz roadster. She could see him back in Eagle Cove as easily as Jessica. Except Jessica had come back, surprising everyone including herself.

Becky turned to the journals, knowing Harry was never coming back to stay.

Integrating the Asian pear was going to require a new approach. The texture would behave like an apple, but the flavoring profile was so much more subtle than anything she'd used before that she hardly knew where to begin. She was halfway to her feet to fetch one so that she'd have the flavor on her tongue as she thought about it, when she remembered that the produce was with her cell phone. In the van parked a mile away. She plummeted back down into the couch and her knee screamed. Crap! She sat very still until the pain eased back down to merely intolerable.

She went back to Volume I.

The first journal covered the pre-beer years, but she flipped through it anyway for nostalgia. Pop had started her off at the age of eight brewing a demijohn of root beer. The five-gallon glass vessel had exploded and nearly killed one of the barn cats. That's how she'd learned about pressure relief valves.

She paged through the learning years. By twelve she made more spending money than most of her friends' allowances selling off her root beer, twenty-five cents a bottle and a nickel back when you returned the glass. Cider and ginger ale had come next. She'd taken over a whole bay of the farm's equipment shed by the time she was sixteen. The second journal contained the years of research on the brewing process. Eventually, there were sketches of the basic system design that she hadn't had a chance to build it until she was twenty.

Pop was frugal and Mom was good with money and they'd trained her well. She never borrowed, never used credit. Becky took no action until she had the cash in hand.

Instead of giving her the money they'd set aside for her college, they gave her the farm in exchange for a ten percent share of profits. They'd taken her college fund and their savings and moved to Alaska. So far all they'd received for their faith in her had been ten percent of the fee she collected for the pasture she rented out for hay; a hundred percent of the brewing money went back into the business. For now.

The second journal ended with the results of her first batch, a simple pilsner. No special flavoring, just a clean, single-fermentation brew.

As she studied the third and fourth journals, she couldn't seem to get comfortable. No matter what she did, her brace was awkward and uncomfortable and her knee throbbed. Every time she thought she had an idea about how to make the Asian pear come to life, a new twinge sent it slipping away.

It was hurting badly by the time she remembered she was supposed to stay ahead of the pain. She popped a pill and tried to cheer it to action before it could possibly have reached her stomach.

Food, she was supposed to have food with it. But again, there was nothing here on the ground floor. She'd never really used the kitchenette, just the mini-fridge for cold sodas.

The recipes in the journals were blurring together. Two bushels in the mash, but scrape off the skins early? Or should she core them to avoid any bitterness from the seeds? Maybe…

There were no maybes. Not until she got the product unloaded and had the malt headed into the mash tun.

But she had no product.

It was in the van.

It would be here soon. It had better be or Jessica was going to be out one brother-in-law and Becky didn't care if it was during her friend's honeymoon.

And when the van finally did show up, she'd need help unloading.

Zander was her best bet. Normally she'd just call Peggy. They went back and forth across the hundred yards separating the barn and Peggy's hangar all the time to give each other a hand lifting a wing, installing a new fermenting tank, or just to share a meal. She was as close to a second mom as a girl could have. But this was getting past friendship and family. There was hard work to be done and there would be more to follow. And if he wasn't available—

She reached for the phone…and swore for the hundredth time today. She couldn't call anyone; her phone was still in the damn van.

When she finally heard the tires crunching on the gravel, she grabbed her crutches and bolted for the door. Then almost did a face plant crossing the high threshold.

From fighting to stay upright her leg was screaming as Harry pulled up in front of her with a wave.

The crutches were wobbling and her knee almost let go despite the brace.

As the van stopped, Becky knew what was about to happen and there was nothing she could do to stop it.

She was about to utterly humiliate herself.

# # #

Harry scrambled but he was too slow.

Becky collapsed to her knees. Tangled in the crutches and with one leg out of commission she went down hard on the grass. The retching sound that ripped from her had him rushing forward.

He pulled her hair clear barely in time and did his best to support her as she heaved long past dry before collapsing against him.

"Wow, Becky." Harry didn't really know what else to say.

"I'm done utterly barfing my guts out now."

"Yeah." He never met a woman who could laugh at herself when she was in complete misery—not that he usually hung around for such moments, but it was still impressive. "Yeah."

"Sure. Fine. Whatever." She flapped a hand indicating the mess she'd just made.

"Nothing a hose won't fix. Let's get you back on the couch," he scooped her up into his arms.

She curled there and he could feel the shivers coursing through her as her body reacted to the abuse. He seemed to be holding and carrying Becky a lot in the last forty-eight hours. He resettled her on the couch, found a damp cloth and a glass of water, but she wouldn't look up at him. While she cleaned up he fetched her toothbrush from upstairs, loaded it up, and handed it to her without comment.

"So," he did his best to keep his tone light, "what was *that* all about?"

"I don't like those pills," she mumbled.

He eyed them and noticed there was only one bottle. "Where are the others?"

"What others?"

He started looking around and found them under the edge of the counter on the far side of the living room as if she'd heaved them there, "These. Anti-nausea."

"Now they tell me."

"With food," he lowered his voice into that I'm-a-lawyer-so-don't-mess-with-me register.

"The only food was upstairs and my knee was hurting too much to try the stairs."

And now he was the one who felt like eight kinds of an idiot. "How long ago?"

"An hour, maybe."

"That means most of it's in your bloodstream," he hoped, he wasn't sure. "Let's give you a buffer of some food anyway."

He went back out to the van and grabbed the bag that the Judge had prepared for him. It had been a real surprise. He'd cleaned up the front of house at the diner as the crowd tailed off, but he really wanted to get back to Becky. However, he didn't want to leave the Judge high and dry again as there was no sign of Peggy.

"Here," his father had held out a bundle of small bills. "Half tips from yesterday and today. Actually one-third from yesterday as I felt that Peggy earned her share."

There'd be no argument from him on that judgment. Harry had riffled through the wad of crumbled green. Nice for a breakfast place he supposed, but not much more than he was paid per hour, which was a quarter of what his firm billed him at per hour. "Greg makes a living on this?"

"He also receives free rent and utilities at the house along with a small salary. And he now serves fancy sit-down dinners Friday and Saturday nights."

Then his father had handed over a bag warm and heavy with food. "Lunch for two. It's a good thing you're doing, helping out Becky."

And his father knew what Harry was doing because there were no secrets in Eagle Cove. He hadn't known what to say other than "Thanks."

On his way back into the barn with lunch, he gathered up her crutches and set them inside the door.

"No!" Becky called out without even raising her head. "Not way over there, Slater."

It took a moment to realize what she'd meant, but it took him no time at all after that to feel like an utter idiot. He'd left her without food and without crutches.

He sat down across from her, "Are you ready for some food?"

Becky smiled at him, "God you are so cute, Slater."

"I am?" He'd earned "handsome" often enough that it had become a meaningless non-sequitur. "Cute" was new.

"I barf my guts out all over you—"

"Actually you missed. Better luck next time."

"—and you have the decency to be the one acting guilty about where you put my crutches."

"But that was unforgiv—"

"Like I said, very cute." She took the to-go container.

Inside were bags of chips and egg salad sandwiches built on thick slices of Cal's sourdough bread. He didn't think after a second morning working at the diner that he'd ever want to face an egg again, but the sandwiches tasted even better than they looked.

"Your dad can make a mean sandwich."

"He can." He also wasn't quite the person that Harry was expecting. He was as gruff and dictatorial as ever with all of his little rules. But he'd also paid Harry for his troubles and it sounded as if he'd worked out a fair deal with Greg. And he really cared how Becky was doing. Not enough to ask outright, but enough to make a nice lunch for her.

"Once we're done eating, I need my cell phone from the van."

"You couldn't even call for help? Shit!" He dropped his sandwich and rushed out to grab it right away. Couldn't he do anything right around Becky?

She took it with a simple, "Thanks. I need to call around and find a pair of hands to hire. Nothing good is happening to all of the supplies in the back of my van by baking them in the sun."

"Who are you—" *Wrong question, Counselor.* "How about if I help you?"

"I thought you were on vacation? Frankly, I kind of expected you to be gone by now. You never visit Eagle Cove for long."

"I'm rather surprised myself." His normal limit was forty-eight hours. Some visits he spent longer in transit than he actually did in Eagle Cove and that suited him just fine. "This trip I don't seem to be in a hurry to leave." He'd actually planned to fly down to Vegas for a couple days and have a hedonistic week before heading back into the grind.

Becky was looking at him and he could see she was thinking hard.

"Penny for your thoughts," he asked her.

"Cheapskate."

"I'm a lawyer. Why are you surprised?"

"A lawyer who drives an SLK350."

"I'm not a stupid lawyer, just a cheapskate."

"Well, I can't pay more than minimum wage. Maybe a bonus for good behavior."

"Good behavior, huh?" He'd certainly liked the way she thought about court orders last night and fines for contempt the night before. "Bonuses sound very tempting."

"This will be really awful for you, so just know you can call it quits at any time and I'll start calling around."

"Deal. Where do we begin?" Her radiant smile of relief was payment enough right there. A beautiful woman who smiled at him like that not because she was manipulating him, but just because he made her happy. It was a hell of a charge to his system.

"Open the big door and back the van in."

# # #

Becky had never appreciated the benefits of having a willing man-servant before. Especially not one who looked so nice after he worked up a sweat and stripped off his t-shirt.

"Whatever you do down there in New Orleans, it suits you well, Counselor," she called from her couch. He was heaving fifty-pound burlap bags of malt and hops out of the van and stacking them in piles by the malt hopper. She hated not having her hands on her own product, but watching a real-life Harry Slater sweat on her behalf was better than Bradley Cooper in the movies.

"Racquetball mostly. Some gym time," he grunted out as he dropped another bag on the pile. And he'd been surprisingly kind after she'd barfed all over him, or at least right in front of him.

Her knee was starting to hurt again. She reached for her crutches and Harry materialized in front of her and squatted down until they were eye to eye.

"What do you need?"

"Well I'm done with that," she waved her hands at the bottles of drugs. "Over the counter for this gal."

"And I'm guessing that they're upstairs, so nope. Put those crutches down."

He was so close that she could smell him. The hint of new clothes from the t-shirt had left him, and there was a small tear in his khakis that he hadn't noticed yet but would probably give him apoplectic fits when he did. He wasn't ugly sweaty, just sort of heated and glowy and smelled so positively male that she wished she could brew a batch with just that heady scent. She wouldn't sell it, she'd just crack a bottle on rare occasions when her spirits needed bolstering after he was gone. His breathing was hard enough from the workout to have his chest and flat gut doing their own beautiful workout. Tempting the fates, she leaned in.

"I'll get them." And he was gone, trotting up the stairs in what he probably thought of as his slumming around shoes, two hundred dollars' worth of Nikes.

He came back down, tossed her a bottle, and kept going.

All she could do was gape. She wanted to be holding a gorgeous chunk of man and instead she was clutching a little white bottle that rattled when she shook it.

Those fates had a nasty sense of humor. She should know that garden gnomes must never tempt the fates.

Of course, Becky Billings wasn't a girl to give up so easily.

# # #

"What's next?" Harry didn't know the last time he'd felt so jazzed. Each of the fifty-pound sacks individually had almost done him in, yet now that they were unloaded and stacked in neat piles, he couldn't wait to do more.

"You've lost your mind."

"I must have," he collapsed back into the armchair and knocked back most of a cold bottle of water that felt so clear and good going down. Water never tasted like that in New Orleans. A cold bottle of water there was bitingly cold in contrast to the thick heat—more likely to give you stomach cramps than soothe a thirsty soul. And as soon as it was out of the refrigerator, it grew thick with condensation that then dripped onto silk ties and Ike Behar suits.

"You are going to be so sore tomorrow."

He flexed and knew she was right, but it didn't mean he wanted to stop.

"The next step starts a process that I have to monitor closely for two to three days. It's not something I can just stop when you decide you get bored. I'd better try to call Zander."

"No. Wait," he rested his hand on hers. She'd already grabbed her cellphone. He always told people in the Big Easy that they knew nothing about moving slow if they hadn't been to small-town coastal Oregon. Becky was the clear exception to that rule. Everything about her was so fast and focused.

"What?"

"Just…" he didn't know why, "…wait. Okay?"

Becky didn't huff in exasperation or roll her eyes. She simply sat like a princess propped on the pillows of her beater couch.

He looked at her for a long time and she let him. Beneath that buxom and flouncy exterior was a very sharp woman. It wouldn't surprise him if she'd assembled every single piece of equipment behind him herself. And maybe done the rebuild upstairs somehow making it comfortable rather than utilitarian. And if he was looking for a woman who was nothing like the sharp-edged women who prowled New Orleans bars and jazz clubs hunting lawyers, doctors, and oil magnates, she was sitting right in front of him.

He should be out of here. He'd timed his arrival Sunday morning to just a few hours before the wedding. It was now Tuesday night, twenty-four hours after his planned departure.

Harry had never considered himself to be a particularly deep guy, but the fact that he hadn't bolted out of town at the first opportunity must mean something. He hadn't caught up with Cal except a little at the wedding. They needed to sit back and crack a few brews. He knew a couple other high school friends still lived in town, maybe more that he didn't know about. Hell, Bethany Garber was as often out of marriages as in them. If he remembered, her social media said that she was over in Salem and between men at the moment. It might be fun to revisit some of that for old time's sake.

But he knew that wasn't why he was still in Oregon.

The reason he was still here was the fragile, broken, beautiful, and tough-as-goddamn-nails woman sitting across from him. Fragile? Who was he kidding? If he hadn't been here, he'd wager that she'd have tackled unloading the van herself despite the drugs and blown knee.

"Your look of angelic innocence and patience isn't fooling anyone, Billings."

"Damn! And I was trying so hard."

But she wasn't. No, erase that. It was clear that she worked harder than anyone he knew. But she made it *look* easy. Around her he felt…good. Like there was hope and purpose above and beyond the daily grind of the law and how far could it be bent. It was a game he excelled at, but one that he'd wager Becky wouldn't like at all.

He wanted…

Just that. He wanted Becky. Not just the way he felt around her, but the way she'd felt against him too.

"Okay. I'd like to cut a deal with the court."

"The court is listening."

"Three days you say?"

Becky nodded.

"Okay. I'm willing to trade three days, except for the hours helping the Judge. My question is: what does the court have to offer in exchange?"

Becky's face remained unreadable as she considered his offer. She always *seemed* to be so open and outgoing and…obvious. Most women were the last no matter how they thought they hid it from him. He could read a blond within three seconds of entering a bar and a brunette before she had time to cast a second glance his way. But he was rapidly learning that Becky Billings was anything but obvious.

What surprised him was quite how much he was vested in her pending answer.

"The court notes," her tone was worthy of any trial judge, maybe even his father, "that she is partially incapacitated by a leg brace."

"So noted and entered in the record."

"The court therefore inquires if the counselor is willing to bear one more burden this evening."

"He's willing to take it under advisement," Harry couldn't stop himself from smiling. No matter the verdict, because it was Becky he knew it would be fun.

"If the counselor would help deliver the court to her bedroom so that she might freshen up, because she rather suspects she smells like a herd of swine, our conference could be continued at a more suitable…" She finally broke and blushed a brilliant red.

"The counselor," who was suddenly having problems with the fit of his slacks, "would like to file a Motion for Change of Venue."

"Passed without objection," Becky managed to gasp out.

Harry strode over and scooped her once more into his arms and headed for the stairs.

"Hey!" She protested.

"What?"

"You're supposed to kiss the court before you drag her away and have your way with her."

"I'll take your pleading under consideration," he continued up the steps. "But due to purported odor similarity to swine, that will take long and careful consideration."

She thumped the side of a fist against his shoulder, then wrapped her arms around his neck and snuggled against him. He buried his nose in her hair as he reached her upstairs apartment. To him she smelled like heaven.

Then he spotted the clawfoot tub and realized that her brace couldn't be immersed.

That meant…a sponge bath. Now that was a judgement he was truly going to enjoy administering.

# Chapter 5

*H*arry's creativity with a wet and soapy sponge had started out incredible and expanded greatly with practice.

For three days he had completely lived up to his word. Together they had made a mash, cooked it, and run it through whirlpool filters and heat exchangers before getting it run into the fermentation tanks.

And the payments had been…breathtaking. She was supposed to be giving payment, not taking it, but her new lover gave her little choice.

Modesty had never been one of her issues, but that first sponge bath had pushed her limits. He'd put a chair in the tub, propped her bad leg on one rim, and then taken what felt like hours to unclothe and wash her. Her beautiful blond hero was meticulous in his investigation of her body. Not a single curve went unwashed or unappreciated. He had caressed, tasted, teased, and cleansed until her breath had sounded in shocky gasps. His research left no place unaddressed from ticklish nibbles on her insteps that had her in whorls of laughter all of the way up to a deep scalp massage and shampoo that had her melting in place.

The towel rub had sent shockwaves through her and after a little experimenting, they'd found a position on the big bed that worked in amazing ways. Since then they'd run through her meager supply of protection and he'd had to make a run for more.

Tuesday night had now rolled into very early Friday morning. She was almost as proficient at horizontal maneuvers as he was and her latest efforts had left both of their bodies humming.

Now she curled against him. Dr. Fairchild had upgraded her from a full leg brace to spending part-time in just a knee brace the prior afternoon which made their present position possible. Her leg now lay across Harry's hips, her head on his chest, and one hand slipped down between his hips and her thigh to cradle him.

"You make a fair brewer's assistant, Counselor Slater."

"As long as you don't move your hand, you'll find no complaints from me."

She lightly massaged him with her fingers and received exactly the groan she'd been hoping for.

"Okay," he gasped out, "you can do that, but only under one condition."

"Name it."

In answer he rolled her onto her back and shifted down to nuzzle her breasts. He certainly did enjoy them and she'd always figured that the main point of having such prominent ones was to have a man nuzzle them.

That or a child.

"What?" Harry looked up. He was so aware of her least little shift in mood.

She hadn't meant to freeze at the unexpected thought. She brushed her hand into his hair and guided him back to what he'd been doing, while her mind went elsewhere.

A child. She'd never particularly thought about it one way or another, at least no more than the next woman. It wasn't a driving force in her life, but she was the age her mother had been when she'd had Becky.

A child. With Harry Slater? Well, that was never going to happen. Over the last three days his suitcase had migrated from the Judge's house to her bedroom, but he'd turned down the dresser drawer she'd offered. She could almost make out the fine leather in the darkness. It sat on a chair close by the bed absolutely declaring the transient nature of this relationship. Was he even aware of what a monogrammed J.W. Hulme distressed leather bag that he insisted was a "duffle" —as if that made a fifteen hundred dollar suitcase more casual—filled with only designer-labeled clothes said about a man? It wasn't that she didn't appreciate fine clothes, it was that he'd come to the coast without a single piece of casual wear.

She'd known all of that going in, so why was she disappointed? Three days was all that he'd promised her and he'd delivered. But that meant that by tonight she might once again be sleeping alone.

He continued to work his way down her body. And between his skill and her affinity for him, her hips were arcing up to press harder against him as her heart drove madly against the inside of her chest.

She might love him, more than might, but this would be no more than a dalliance for the high-powered lawyer. In a matter of weeks Becky would be no more than a good last-trip-home memory. In a few months she probably wouldn't even be that.

But for the moment, this wonderful ecstatic moment of raw joy, she gave herself completely and knew that she would treasure it forever. This time the waves slamming through her body rose as much from her heart as from her hips.

# # #

Harry lay with his face pressed into Becky's stomach. One hand was trapped beneath her buttock when she'd finally collapsed back onto the bed. With the other he reached up to gently massage the nicest breast he'd ever held. Her good leg, which had latched across his back as she rode over her peak, was still draped lazily around him.

He no longer asked what he was doing here.

What was the point of asking? He'd be gone soon.

He couldn't invite Becky to go with him. He'd seen her as they worked the brewing process. Her passion for this place that she'd built with her own hands was as undeniable as the passion she brought to their sex. She'd spent hours poring over her recipe books and making notes as carefully as he'd ever studied precedent when building a case. They really did look like alchemy texts: the leather worn by a thousand handlings, the pages covered margin to margin in Becky's draftsman-quality lettering. He could read it easily, not that the words made much sense. "Overly dense wort." "Excess raffinose production in lager about 12 degrees C." "Dusty mouthfeel with acetaldehyde foreground and catty aftertaste."

There was nothing here for him. It had been fun, though he would never be more than a mediocre assistant. He'd called in for another week of vacation and, since they owed him several months of untaken leave, they hadn't argued for long. He'd just come off a large case and didn't have anything on his desk that one of the junior associates assigned to him couldn't handle.

But he hadn't told Becky about the extra week. He could see she was involved, more every day. She was a decent and fair woman and hadn't once referred to any future in their relationship, but she must be thinking it.

"That…"

Harry pushed his face deeper into her belly. He didn't want to hear it. Every time she spoke he braced himself, trying to be ready for the shoe to drop.

"That was absolutely spectacular, Counselor. I'll return the favor if my heart rate ever drops back down below stratospheric." She languidly shifted and moved against him, somehow snuggling him tighter against her.

Her fingers began playing with his hair and he groaned. It felt so good that he never wanted her to stop.

No. He definitely couldn't tell her about the extra week. If they were like this after three days, what would it be like after ten?

Vegas. He'd go back to his original plan of Vegas. Pick up a showgirl or a recent divorcée and purge Eagle Cove and Becky Billings from his blood.

Greg would be back tonight and making one of his fancy dinners at the diner. Harry would take Becky out for a special dinner, let her know it had been a wonderful time, and be gone in the morning.

He could work with that.

Becky's breathing shifted, the rise and fall of her flat stomach against his cheek slowing until he knew she was asleep. He now knew her mood by how she breathed or smiled or laughed. He knew that she sang when she was happiest, making them a meal while balancing on crutches in the kitchen or working at even the most mundane chores. That her world narrowed to such a tight focus when she was working on her brewing that her singing stopped and the rest of the world ceased to exist. He'd tried to seduce her while the heat exchanger was…exchanging heat or whatever it did. He'd had no luck until the whole batch had been safely moved through and into the CCV fermentation tanks and a proper dose of yeast added.

The instant the temperature was set she had jumped him and they'd ultimately done it like animals gone mad right against the still warm curves of the copper kettle.

There was one other thing he knew as he lay against Becky in the midnight darkness; he was utterly, completely, and most of all metaphorically screwed.

# Chapter 6

*Harry knew he still* had a smile on his face when he reached The Puffin Diner at precisely five minutes to six to help with breakfast service—pushing the limits, but still on time.

Becky had insisted on paybacks when his alarm went off, but had respected his limited schedule. By habit he didn't wake quickly and his body hadn't completely shifted to Oregon time. By the time the snooze alarm buzzed, she'd teased a part of him to life and he became fully awake already deep inside her. Midway through, a frantic slap at the clock bought him another nine minutes. She kissed him as their bodies struggled to get closer than was physically possible, and she didn't stop. Her tongue was ravaging his mouth just as thoroughly as he was ravaging her in other places.

She swallowed his groan as the release slammed through him. He knew it was a good one for her because when he got it especially right, she didn't moan, she hummed. Literally. He'd never been able to pick out the tune, but the stronger it was, the happier she was. He could feel it where her breasts pressed hard against his chest. Her powerful, working-woman's, and thankfully with close-cut fingernails, hands dug into the muscles along his shoulder blades as she hung on for the ride that coursed through her body.

He'd barely finished shuddering out his last when she finally eased back a half-inch, "You're going to be late, Counselor." And then she rolled free and was gone from the bed.

He'd lain there dazed past speech as he watched her hobble over and take a quick sponge bath. By the time the second snooze jolted him to action, she was already over in the kitchen making herself a protein shake and still wearing nothing but her leg brace.

It was a sight he could watch all day. Then he checked his watch. He could watch all day only if he wanted to make the Judge even more prickly than he typically was. In fact, he'd had to hurry enough that it had left very little time to enjoy the scenery before he had to bolt out the door.

A classic September coastal drizzle greeted him, but he was too late to turn back for his jacket which was upstairs. If he did go back inside to fetch it, he'd see Becky wandering about her apartment as if all goddesses did indeed grace the earth with their nakedness. Worse, he might see her dressed in her jeans and flannel shirt and be faced with the choice of whether or not to get her back out of them. Instead, he slogged through the mud and managed to get into his rental car without stepping in any puddles that might soak his sneakers.

He was shivering by the time he came in the back door of the diner. His shirt clung to him and his hair was dripping. He'd completely forgotten about coastal microclimates. The distance from the shore to Becky's place was a difference of barely a mile. Yet a light drizzle there was a deluge here.

The Judge was at his griddle and the air was thick with bacon and coffee. He eyed Harry carefully before stating, "No Oregonian is ever caught without a jacket."

"And no goddamn New Orleans' lawyer would ever need to remember that."

The Judge regarded him a moment longer, then turned back to his griddle.

Peggy was also there.

Harry's first reaction was to be pissed. The old man had his phone number and could have called to say he already had help. Harry could still be warm, dry, and in bed with the sexiest woman he'd ever laid hands on. Could have taken the time to show her just how much he appreciated her.

Peggy was hunched over the old waffle iron. Damn thing hadn't worked in years, what was so important about fixing it now, that she couldn't have covered breakfast service? Every menu had a wavy black line drawn through "Waffles (with blueberries when in season)" so it wasn't like there was a sudden rush.

"Need some parts," Peggy closed it back up and was gone before Harry had a chance to protest.

"Time," the Judge intoned like his griddle was a judicial bench. Harry was surprised he didn't rap his spatula on the cast iron like a gavel. He'd retired five years back from the judgeship up in Newport. Since then he'd run the diner in the mornings, held office hours—mostly for weddings and wills—in the afternoons, and took weekends off. Five years off the bench and he still—

This time he did bang the spatula, making the metal ring loudly enough to hurt Harry's ears and make him jump.

Harry grabbed an apron and order pad, turning on lights as he moved toward the front of house. He stopped to turn on the coffee pot to set the first pot brewing. He could feel the Judge's eyes boring into him as he did so, even though there wasn't a soul waiting on the porch. The big clock said six-oh-three when he unlocked the front door and flicked on the porch lights.

" 'Bout time," Cal grunted as he pushed through the front door.

"Eat shit, buddy."

Cal merely grinned in response and made a point of clipping him hard shoulder-to-shoulder as he passed by. Cal Mason Jr. was the size of a Mack truck—several inches taller and wider than Harry. How he'd been so fast on his feet back when the two of them had ruled the Puffling soccer team was still a mystery. His big frame meant that his brush against Harry had sent him stumbling backward and crashing into a table.

"Oops! Did you run into me? That always happens with little people. They run into me and just kinda bounce back off. So sorry." He almost delivered the whole line with a straight face, but it slid off sideways into a self-satisfied grin that had Harry bracing to commit a charging penalty in turn.

Cal moved aside fast enough to get clear without looking like he was hurrying before Harry had a chance to untangle himself from the chairs he'd collapsed into. Cal continued blithely toward his standard spot at the counter. Cal's day had started hours earlier at the Blackbird Bakery across the street and he was always first in for breakfast as soon as the lights were on.

The Judge would have his standard order ready, but wouldn't serve it up until Harry hung a ticket. He scribbled "Cal" across a ticket, tore it off, stuck it in the spinner, and turned it to face his father.

"Junior or senior?"

As if the Judge wasn't less than five feet from Cal because Cal always sat at the counter that faced the service window.

Harry spun the ticket back and yanked it free. A corner of the ticket tore off. The bit fluttered down and managed to land in the mug of coffee Harry had already poured for Cal. He dumped the coffee down the service sink, but splashed a lot of it on his Nikes. The blazing hot liquid ran right through the mesh and caused him to yelp at the sudden sting.

He slashed "Jr" across the ticket and managed to not write, "Asshole!" as well, stuck it back in the spinner, and slapped it around to face his father. The Judge slid across the plate with what might have been a smile—as if the man ever smiled.

Harry grabbed the plate, adding a seared hand to his morning's complaints, but slung it across the gap anyway and nearly dumped the Western omelet, hash browns, bacon, and English muffin in Cal's lap.

"Smooth, buddy. Real damn smooth. Did you forget everything I ever taught you about how to handle a hot ball?"

Before Harry could come up with a good comeback, he always found that hard when he knew his father was listening, Ralph Baxter came in with seven tourists. Must be an early start to a fishing trip. He tried to remember what was running in late September and came up mostly blank. Cod? Halibut? Was salmon still running?

Whatever it was, Jessica's father was one of the best fishermen on the coast and there'd be a lot of happy tourists by end of day. Happy people spent more around the town which was good for Eagle Cove and…

And why the hell was he wasting a single brain cell on this sad little place? Rather than attacking his father or Cal, Harry grabbed a fistful of menus and stalked off.

"Smile," Cal whispered as Harry walked past him.

"Fine!" He plastered one on and turned back to Cal. "Better?"

"Sure, if you want them to think you're going to kill them rather than serve them."

Harry tried to take a deep breath to ease down. He knew that Eagle Cove always made him crazy. Another breath.

It wasn't working.

He gave up on the smile and figured he'd let the tourists dine here at their own risk.

### # # #

Becky wished she could think of something other than Harry. He'd marked her property more thoroughly than any dog worried about the sanctity of his fire hydrant. And she knew it was completely unintentional. Worse, that he wasn't even aware of it.

The beautiful leather suitcase on the chair in her bedroom. A couple of shirts and the Michael Kors suit he'd worn to the wedding—the gray of a spring sky just before a long-awaited rain—hung at the end of her closet bar. Toothbrush and hairbrush at the sink. A second towel air-drying beside hers near the tub.

The tub had made her blush every time she looked at it after the first day that they became lovers. She'd never been one to parade around unclothed, not even when she was alone. But after that first sponge bath, modesty had seemed out of place.

Harry had taken right to it, complimenting her open floor plan. As if she'd meant it that way. She had just been being cost-efficient. Interior walls took planning to lay out the rooms and then time and money to build, wire, and finish. They also made a place feel smaller and the room wasn't that spacious to begin with. She could expand to the whole loft, but couldn't imagine why she'd ever need it.

A family someday?

Sure, maybe in some other century.

Living alone in a renovated hayloft she'd dropped in four walls and a ceiling and called it good. Her closet was a heavy wood dowel hung from screw eyes in the ceiling by some old rope.

Going to pee the first time would have been mortifying, except for the way Harry looked at her. With him watching as she crutched her way from bed to bath, she'd felt beautiful rather than like her usual garden gnome. She knew he liked her curves, but over the last three days his attention had shifted more and more often to her face as she stumped around the apartment with all the grace of a lumberjack.

Once they'd spent the desires of their bodies, they'd spent hours in bed, on the downstairs sofa, or just sitting on the bench outside her front door when the sun warmed it, and talked. Often about nothing at all, just leaning together and chatting about the day, old friends, and new dreams. In retrospect it had been about *her* new dreams. Maybe slick, successful lawyers didn't dream about the future.

Maybe he didn't have to.

He'd soon be full partner at a prestigious law firm. All dug in with his high-rise condo and fancy sports car. He talked about cases, all corporate law now. Defending construction contractors and large corporations against the inevitable actions brought against them. His firm handled the cases that were too big and messy for their own in-house counsel. Sometimes guilty and sometimes innocent, it was his job to defend them and it sounded to her uneducated ear as if he did it well. It also sounded as if it wasn't much fun, but who was she to judge someone else's choices. She'd chosen being a brewer over college and wherever that might have led.

He'd left reminders of himself everywhere. The tub, the bed, the couch downstairs, even in the brewery…he'd left behind memories as deep and thick as an unfiltered stout.

Once she'd managed to crutch her way downstairs, she brushed a hand over the copper kettle. No man had ever even kissed her in her brewery. Now and forevermore she'd think of how their shared cries had tangled among the equipment as he'd taken her hard against this now cool metal. Every batch she cooked would incorporate the memory.

She was so pathetic.

How could she possibly think that they'd be good memories after he was gone? How many batches of beer and cider would she flavor with tears?

"None, Becky Billings! Not a single, solitary one!"

She listened and didn't like what she heard.

Instead she strapped on the big walking brace that would keep her knee immobilized, then fished out the long-handled brush and a hot-water hose to clean up the equipment in preparation for the next cooking. Perhaps a ginger stout with some of the leftover Asian pear as a sweetener.

Even over the thumping of the high-pressure pump she could still hear the echoes of their passion.

"No tears, Billings," she tried to drown out the echoes with little luck.

She turned to her work, but it was a long time before she felt any of the usual peace doing the task.

# # #

Peggy swung back through and finished tinkering with the waffle iron.

The Judge watched her intently, almost as if she was hurting him rather than helping him. He was so focused on her that he botched a couple of orders that Harry silently slid back across the service window for a re-do.

When Peggy finished, she'd patted the Judge's shoulder with an easy familiarity before leaving again.

The Judge's idea of a lowered voice carried easily across any room, but this time Harry barely heard the old man when he sighed and spoke to himself, "Well, that's that then."

Then looking up, he caught Harry watching him.

"Waffles will be back on the menu come Monday," he made it sound unimportant, but Harry could see that it worried him.

Unable to ask why, Harry simply nodded in acknowledgement and moved off to bus some more tables. Monday would be Greg's concern, not his.

The crowd was thinning before Harry thought to add his own name to his brother's dinner reservation sheet. He'd taken any number of calls during the week, but it wasn't until he was staring at the page on the clipboard that he began to be impressed.

How many people had he already told on the phone that both of tonight's seatings were already sold out?

Sold out. Two seatings.

There was no menu, but he'd seen the jar with the sign that simply said, "Fifty Dollars. Drinks included. Tips welcome."

Fifty dollars a person was high on the coast. He could think of only a few other places anywhere along the shore that charged more. Yet his little brother didn't lack for reservations.

But he'd wanted to bring Becky here.

He turned to the next sheet. Saturday's first seating was gone as well. On the second seating he scribbled his name down and put a "2" after it. Only space for one more couple.

"Sweet!" Greg looked over his shoulder.

Harry startled at Greg's sudden appearance, then hit his brother on the head with the clipboard.

"What the hell are you still doing here?" Greg thumped him on the arm—hard enough for it to be payback for being hit with the clipboard rather than a friendly greeting. "I was sure you'd be gone before I got back."

"Old man trapped me." Then he glanced past Greg. "You don't look so good, Jessica."

"I don't?" She was raising her hand to her fair complexion.

"Nope. You look absolutely incredible," he brushed Greg aside much the way Cal had shoved him this morning, and pulled Jessica into a brief hug, then he stepped back again.

Her light blond hair was highlighted with droplets from the rain. Her blue eyes were sparking with joy and her smile was huge. She'd always had a killer smile, but it was over the top now. She positively shone against the backdrop of the gray day going on outside the window. She was sleek and slender unlike Becky's generous curves, but she…

"You do look amazing. How in the hell is that possible? I mean you married my little brother, after all."

"I'm just continuing an old family tradition."

"That," Harry puzzled at it for a few seconds, "doesn't make any sense at all."

Greg just grinned at him, "Oh, but it does."

"Come on and I'll tell you and the Judge together," she nodded toward the kitchen.

Harry turned to check on the patrons. No one else had snuck in while he was distracted. It was just ten minutes to the ten o'clock end of service and the few remaining guests were all served. He followed Greg and Jessica back into the kitchen.

The Judge waved a spatula in greeting to Greg and Jessica, but didn't leave the grill.

"Judge," Jessica smiled up at him.

He tipped his head to show that he was listening.

"You know my family tradition."

"Seems that I do," he checked under the edge of an omelet but decided to let it be for the moment.

"Some parts of it are repeating, and no, I'm not going to be divorcing your son."

Jessica's mother had married Ralph Baxter four times and divorced him three, without ever moving out of the house. If it wasn't that…

Harry didn't know what was happening, but Jessica now had the Judge's full attention.

"Are you…" he trailed off.

Harry had never known the Judge to be at a loss for words.

Jessica simply nodded and smiled. No, she nodded and glowed. Not only did she look incredibly happy, she also…

Greg leaned close and whispered, "Her mom got pregnant the week before the wedding, though she didn't realize it at the time. We started trying, but didn't expect it to happen so fast."

Harry was still having trouble adjusting to Greg and Jessica being married. And now she was pregnant and—

"How do you like the sound of Uncle Harry?"

At a complete loss for how else to respond, he punched Greg in the arm hard enough to send him flailing into the big steel door of the walk-in refrigerator.

The Judge's response was wholly unexpected. He stepped up to Jessica and wrapped her into his arms as if he was holding something precious. The Judge didn't hug people, ever. But he hugged Jessica Baxter.

Harry shook his head to clear it, but it didn't help.

Then Greg's counterstrike caught him hard enough on the shoulder to send him tumbling out through the swinging door to land on the dining room floor.

Greg stuck his head out and grinned, "You've got customers."

Harry looked up into the face of Cal's father. Cal Sr. looked down at him with a stony gaze. The water dripping off the brim of his hat pattered in Harry's face.

"Tall stack and coffee if you're done lying around, boy." Then he turned and headed to his favorite table. The way he'd said it took Harry right back to high school days.

Cal Sr. was more of a father figure than the Judge had ever been. That wasn't quite right Harry thought as he climbed to his feet and dusted himself off. He'd been a more *active* father figure. As coach of the soccer team, he'd had an eye on things that the Judge didn't due to his commute an hour each way four days a week up to the Newport courtroom.

The first time Harry had felt up a girl, Cal Sr. had somehow known. He'd hauled both his and Jr.'s ass out on his fishing skiff and lectured them but good on what he'd do if they ever went all the way with a girl without protection. After scaring the crap out of both of them, he'd handed each a box of condoms.

His first sick drunk, Sr. had once again hauled him out onto the glaring water on sixteen-feet of rocking aluminum. It had been an abuse that had his eyes, head, and gut vying for the title of Most Willing to Die First.

"Did you touch a girl in this state?"

"Girls didn't want anything to do with me."

"More sense that I thought they had. Good for them. You make stupid mistakes when you're drunk. Doing them to yourself is one thing, doing them to another, that's not right." Then Sr. gave the drunk driving lecture even though neither Harry nor Jr. had their license yet.

And when he and Jr. had been star forward strikers for the Puffling soccer team and didn't think, but both *knew* they were better than gods, Sr. hadn't said a single word in praise. That was perhaps the hardest lesson and one that Harry had taken years to understand. "Being good is one thing. Being good enough that others say it without you saying it first is what counts."

He filled out Cal Sr.'s order and spun it in.

The Judge handed the plate across, already made up.

Harry delivered it without comment to Sr. and received not a word back, just a nod of thanks.

"Seriously, bro," Greg popped up at his elbow once more.

Little shit had always been able to do that to him. Even that first time Harry had kissed Jessica when they were both fifteen—Greg had just happened to check the widow's walk of the Lamont's B&B at that moment. Partly because they had never been able to get clear of Greg it hadn't gotten far enough for him to earn Sr's "feel up versus fuck" lecture about Jessica; that had come later.

"Why're you still in town?" He tugged the order pad out of Harry's apron pocket, scribbled down a pair of orders, clipped and spun them around to the Judge himself.

"Dad needed help."

"Like that would be enough to make you stay in Eagle Cove for an extra five minutes." Greg filled a coffee mug and made a hot chocolate with marshmallows and carried them to a table where Jessica was just sitting down. So much for the Judge's "only children get marshmallows" rule.

Harry followed along with two sets of silverware and napkins, "I was also helping Becky."

"Since when," Jessica asked, "did Becky Billings need help with anything. I swear she is the most capable woman on the planet. I find her completely daunting."

"Since she blew out her knee. I've been her hands and strong back all week."

Greg choked on his coffee. "You? When was the last time you did manual labor?"

"All week, asshole."

Jessica was on her feet and clutching onto his forearm. "She was hurt? Where is she now?"

"Out at the brewery. She's fine."

"I gotta go!" She looked desperately at Greg.

He tossed her a set of car keys and she bolted for the door.

"Jessica," the Judge's voice boomed out bringing her to a screeching halt.

It was the same tone that had electrified Harry with raw terror every single time. He remembered his last Christmas visit home at twenty-two. He'd been upstairs in his room working on his undergraduate thesis, when his name had rung through the old Victorian. He'd almost lost his laptop to the floor as he'd jolted off the bed in a cold sweat wondering what the hell he'd done wrong this time. He'd raced downstairs only to have the Judge ask him to hold some boards so that he could cut them more easily.

Jessica didn't look the least mortified, though Harry could feel an adrenal shock just as a by-blow from standing nearby the Judge's call.

"Here," the Judge slid across a pair of to-go containers. "Greg, I'll have to recook yours, give me a minute."

"Thanks, Judge," Jessica waved and bolted out the door.

" I, uh," Harry looked back at Greg and tried to remember what they'd been talking about. He never lost the thread of a testimony or cross-examination. He could pick up a thread days later that the jury had forgotten all about and impress the hell out of them with his masterful understanding of such a complex case.

"Why you're still here?" Greg helped him out as he settled back in his chair.

"Right. I couldn't leave the old man to himself, could I?"

Cal Sr. was eyeing him from a nearby table, almost as if he didn't recognize Harry all of a sudden. Was it so damn weird that he'd lent a hand where it was needed?

"And Becky was really hurt and drugged senseless on major painkillers." And fun as hell. Somehow the morning had been so busy that it slipped by without her really being in his thoughts. But she'd still sort of…been there. *Again with the words, Counselor.* He could practically hear her tease and it made him smile.

Right up until the moment Greg's fist crashed into his jaw and sent him falling into Cal Sr.'s lap. The old man put a hand on his back and heaved him toward Greg hard enough to hurt.

Greg got right up in his face, "You fucked Becky Billings while she was on painkillers?" His roar stilled the diner. There wasn't so much as a fork clink. The latest pot of coffee brewing broke the silence with that dry-sucking burble when the coffeemaker had sprayed the last of its water on the grounds.

"No, I didn't!" Harry roared back at Greg as soon as he caught his breath.

Greg remained poised with both fists clenched.

"Goddamn it!" Harry rubbed at his jaw.

It hurt like hell.

"What we…did," he really didn't enjoy announcing it to the whole world. It had been something private between them. More than that, it had been precious and now it was sullied by his little shit of a brother.

Greg shifted his weight, readying another blow. Harry was so goddamn sick of everyone pushing him around today that he'd welcome it right now.

"Why the hell couldn't you have stayed on your goddamn honeymoon until I was gone? What we did was *after* she was off the drugs and it was very, very mutual. And then I spent the week busting my ass to help her because she asked nicely. Now you can go and fetch your own damn breakfast, asshole."

Harry peeled off the apron, and jammed it into Greg's hands, barely resisting the urge to paste him in the jaw. Instead he shoved him at Cal Sr.—hard!

Sr. slid his chair out of the way and let Greg tumble by to crash into another table, one still filled with dirty dishes which clattered to the floor and broke. Water glasses tumbled and shattered as chairs skittered away to knock into other patrons' tables.

Harry took one look back at the Judge who offered the same neutral expression every single time his sons fought.

To hell with both of them.

Sr. again had that look as if he didn't recognize Harry standing right in front of him. Then he smiled slowly as if inordinately pleased with some inner reflection.

To hell with all three of them.

Harry slammed his way out the front door and strode into the chill September rain.

# # #

"Did he really?"

Becky could only laugh with delight. She so loved having Jessica back in town after the fourteen years she'd been living in Chicago.

"He did. Right over there," Becky pointed at the copper cooking kettle. "I never knew how wonderful it was to make a man lose all control because he's so desperate to have you."

Jessica's smile was huge in turn, "Isn't it though."

They worked their way through a pair of the Judge's smoked salmon omelets as they sat side by side on the couch.

She remembered the first time Harry had sat there while they ate burgers from the Plover. The sweetness of that kiss, so warm, soft, and gentle. And no matter how hard she'd worked her hands and body—which her knee was really complaining about despite wearing the full brace all morning—she hadn't been able to block the thoughts about Harry and how soon he'd be gone from her life. And—

Before she knew what was happening, Jessica had set their to-go containers on the small table then slid close to wrap her arms around Becky.

Becky buried her face in her best friend's shoulder.

"He's never going to stay here. And he knows that it would be like ripping out a piece of my heart to ask me to leave."

"I know. You so belong here."

"It doesn't help to have that confirmed. I swore I wasn't going to cry over him." Which was a completely pointless statement as she was now weeping and couldn't seem to stop it.

She could feel Jessica's nod, "I said the same thing."

"It doesn't work," she barely managed to choke out, "does it?"

"Nope," and Jessica ran a soothing hand  up and down Becky's back.

She'd thought that barfing her guts out at Harry's feet had been the worst, but this pain was unending and there was no solution except to give up everything she loved. "And that's if he even wants me," it came out as a sob and more tears.

Jessica pushed her back until they were face to face, "If he doesn't realize that you're the most incredible woman on the planet—"

"Besides you!" Jessica always looked so slender and perfect.

"Well, of course me," Jessica's smile was warm and teasing. "If he doesn't realize that you're the second most incredible woman on the planet—"

"And Natalya!" Jessica's cousin was the darkly sexy version of the blond beauty currently holding her.

"Becky!" Jessica gave her a shake. "You are beautiful and incredible and have done amazing things. If Harry doesn't know that you're the best thing he's ever going to find, then he's an idiot. And if you don't get that about yourself…well, shit! You scare the crap out of Natya and me all the time."

"I do?" Becky liked the sound of that though she couldn't imagine how it was possible.

"Duh! Look at this!" Jessica waved a hand at the brewery. "You did this. I managed to create a failed journalism career and I'm now trying not to weep with terror as I scrape through my startup year as the town's marketing manager. An effort, I'll remind you, that is partly funded by Becky Billings BlueBird Brewery."

"But you're great at it. I knew you would be. You can do anything."

"Hello!" Jessica waved at the brewing equipment again.

And Becky looked at it, really looked. Over two thousand gallons of beer were working their way through the fermentation tanks. A line of bright steel kegs, filled and ready for delivery, were lined up along the wall. She'd have to figure out how to do deliveries, because they were due to go out next week for Tillamook down to Coos Bay and two new clients inland in Eugene.

She'd dreamed a dream when she was an eight-year-old girl and it was real. Right there. In front of her. She turned back to Jessica.

"Hello!" Jessica waved again at the brewery.

Becky nodded. "Right. So…if Harry doesn't get what he's missing then…" she wasn't ready, couldn't bring herself to say to hell with him. "Then…" she still didn't know what was on the other side of that statement.

"Then," Jessica grinned at her, "we'll just have to make sure he figures it out."

She had no idea how to do that, but she liked the way it sounded.

"Now," Jessica gave her a napkin to wipe her eyes with, "I happen to know exactly what you need." She pulled out her phone and began dialing.

# # #

Harry was a hundred feet from the Slater Victorian when a car headed into town splashed to a halt beside him.

Gina Lamont, Natalya's mom and Jessica's aunt, rolled down the window.

"Do you need a ride, Harry? Where's your coat?"

"Forgot it. I'm almost there."

"You sure?"

He looked into the car. Gina was a tall, statuesque redhead and beside her sat a smaller woman who gave the impression of being almost entirely made up of flowing light brown hair. Gina wore a stylish rain jacket and the other woman was dressed in a well-worn yellow slicker and a rain hat with a wide enough brim to mostly hide her face.

"I'm fine."

"Okay. Take a hot shower quick." Gina rolled up her window and drove away.

Harry made it five more steps before he stumbled to a halt ankle deep in a mud puddle. He'd stopped caring about how wet he was before he had even turned off Beach Way. He kept his hands jammed in his pockets and his shoulders hunched against the on-going deluge. Another two degrees colder and he'd be shivering. He was just warm enough to be totally, completely miserable.

He came to a halt when he realized that he'd been aimed to the wrong place. And he'd been in such a head-down, foul mood that he'd walked two miles in the rain before he noticed. He had no clothes here at his childhood home, they were all out at Becky's. He'd go to the guest house and steal one of Greg's jackets for the long walk back to town to fetch his car.

Except their house was locked. He looked at the sodden driveway. Greg's truck was parked in the carport. And he'd seen Jessica take off from the diner in a ten-year-old VW Beetle. There were no recent tracks in the mud, meaning Jessica and Greg were only just returning from their short honeymoon. He trudged across the yard but the big house was locked as well.

Putting his head down he turned and slogged back toward town.

Now, when he needed a ride, no one passed along the lane. It was as if the town had emptied with the gray Friday morning.

That reminded him that there was a rhythm to a small coastal town. Friday morning is when everyone did their shopping and other errands so that they didn't have to fight the weekend tourists who would start cluttering up the store aisles by two or three in the afternoon. So everyone would be out for a while, then they come streaming back but all going in the wrong direction.

Sure enough, he was most of the way back to town when the first cars passed him, heading out of town not into it. Each older person waved. One or two of the high school-age ones who were headed home for lunch aimed at the mud puddles, sending huge gouts of cold muddy spray his way. He'd done the same himself as a kid. When you saw a tourist being as stupid as he was, they were marked as fair game.

Paybacks were hell.

He and Becky had made a whole game out of paybacks. Those hadn't been hell. They'd been the best time he'd had in—

He stumbled to a halt in front of The Puffin Diner. It was almost noon and the windows were dark. He splotched muddy footprints from his ruined Nikes up the steps and across the porch.

Locked.

He trudged around to the back.

Locked.

By shading the glass he could just make out where the apron he'd worn all morning hung. In the pocket were his car keys. After that final round this morning of feeling up a naked Becky as she leaned back against the kitchen counter and moaned like a lost soul, he'd been running so late that the keys had still been in his hands as he'd grabbed the apron. It had been natural to dump them in one of the pockets.

He turned around to stare at his rental car.

It was pointless, but he went down to check it anyway.

Big city habits, he'd locked it.

The joke on the coast was that you locked your car only during zucchini season. It was so that local gardeners didn't slip in a couple of the overgrown monsters that they didn't have the heart to compost.

He looked up Beach Way. No one to ask for a ride really.

Cal was a possibility, but Sr.'s truck was parked close beside Jr.'s and he didn't think he could take more of the old man's disapproving looks right at the moment. God forbid if he had some lecture on tap this morning.

Harry had already walked two miles out to the house and two back. One more mile to Becky's wasn't going to kill him.

It only felt as if it would.

He considered calling her, but then she'd probably feel obliged to come fetch him in her van and he didn't want her driving with that knee yet. Besides, he could see his phone right there, on the locked car's dash.

He pulled up the sodden collar of his Peter Millar sport shirt and began trudging out of town.

# # #

Jessica had been absolutely right, this is exactly what she needed.

The brewery was alive with a dozen knitters. Every Tuesday and Friday afternoon, everyone who was available met out at Gina's lovely B&B for knitting. Tuesday Becky had been drugged out of her mind. No, she'd been off the drugs by then, and busy admiring Harry unloading her truck. Then the sponge bath and… She'd been busy.

So, this afternoon wasn't as good as last Tuesday's, but it was wonderful in every other way.

Today, the ladies of the town had brought their knitting group to her. They pulled chairs and stools out of the tasting room and made a merry circle with the couch and armchair. She'd had Jessica pull out a case of cider and another of a cream soda she was rather proud of. Gina had brought ham-and-turkey roll-ups. Monica supplied veggies and hummus. And Becky had sent Tiffany up to her apartment to raid her secret stash of a giant bag of Fritos. Tiffany had chortled with glee and the two of them feasted on their newfound shared passion for crunchy salt and high fat content.

The saga of her leg was the first topic as everyone pulled out their knitting projects. She herself was working on a scarf of a ridiculously sparkly and floofy yarn of gold, reds, and oranges.

"It is autumn after all," she defended her choice to the traditionalists in the group who poo-pooed "novelty" yarn. She'd chosen an eyelash yarn which had a thousand little strands sprouting from the main thread like brilliant fireworks. It was fun, ticklish, and it was very easy to imagine teasing Harry's body with it because it was so soft. Not that the scarf would be done before he was gone, but it was still nice to imagine.

"Harry? He's really helping out?" Marjorie Winslow's question was enough to shock the multiple conversations into a single ply.

"He was always such a cocky boy, no pun intended." Gina said it in such a way that it was obvious that the pun was wholly intended which earned her a round of laughter.

The whole town must know that the two of them were shacked up together, but still Becky couldn't stop the blush that led to catty calls for details.

"No," Becky defended him. "He's not. Except in the way you actually mean it of course."

Gina threw her head back and unleashed one of her big laughs. It was a good offset to Becky's earlier tears on Jessica's shoulder.

"Seriously though," Marjorie Winslow, who had been the best second-grade teacher ever born, narrowed her eyes in concern, "I remember him as a rather arrogant boy."

A murmur of agreement rose.

As the younger women told different tales of when he'd tried to date them, or the older ones of when he'd gone after one of their daughters, Becky had her own memories to think over. She hadn't done that much, being too wrapped up in enjoying the present.

With a senior class of only thirty-four students, it was hard not to know everything about everyone. Yet even in so small a group, her and Harry's circles rarely overlapped outside the classroom. Even in retrospect, she saw less of the arrogant boy and more of someone trying to prove himself to the world.

The Judge was such an austere and powerful man, it was hard to imagine what it would have been like growing up as his eldest son. He set such a high standard to live up to. And that had been contrasted with his wife. Ma Slater, as absolutely everyone called her until finally that's how she began signing her paintings, had been a reserved yet warm woman. She was someone that you could take your troubles to and always receive good advice. If Becky hadn't had Peggy living so nearby, she'd have missed Harry's mother badly.

Now that Becky knew the man grown, she could see the elements of his past so clearly.

"No," she interrupted a particularly ribald story. "He isn't arrogant anymore. He's…lovely."

As if on cue, the front door slammed open and an apparition trudged through the door. Harry was drenched, covered in mud, and visibly shivering.

Dumping her knitting out of her lap, she raced over to him as fast as she could wearing the leg brace.

"Are you okay?"

He looked at her out of haunted eyes. Filled with a pain so deep that she almost recognized it as her own.

# # #

Harry glanced over Becky's head at the circle of women who had frozen in place at his entrance. He was greeted by a wide variety of expressions. Some smiling, Jessica the most prominent among them. Some scowling, led by the town's terror of a second grade teacher—given a choice, Marjorie Winslow was one woman he would *not* want to catch up with while visiting Eagle Cove. Gina and her sister Monica looked amused. And the one he'd seen in the car with Gina, the woman with the long flow of wavy brunette hair, just watched him carefully—as carefully as he'd ever watched a key witness. Not judging, but not trusting either.

"Are you okay, Harry?" Becky rested a hand on his forearm but snatched it back from the wet and cold.

"So not." Standing still he was starting to shiver. "Looks like the jury hasn't reached a consensus on me yet either." He kept his voice low.

Becky glanced over at the circle of women as they began to return to their knitting but were clearly paying attention to the drama unfolding by the door.

"Of course we have," Gina Lamont called out proving he hadn't kept his voice low enough. "Off with his head!"

"Great." He wasn't sure that he'd argue the verdict at this point himself. He began peeling off his shoes and socks so that he didn't track the mud all through Becky's place.

Becky reached out again and he stepped back.

"No. I'm disgusting." And he hadn't meant it quite the way it came out, but it had been a long, wet mile from town. And his thoughts had become as sodden as his underwear. He didn't want Vegas. He didn't want some needy, leggy blond trying to prove she was still attractive fresh off a divorce. He wanted this stunning, amazing, pint-sized woman standing not three feet away.

And what was he going to do about that?

He was going to take her out to dinner tomorrow night (only because he couldn't get a reservation sooner), and then leave her on Sunday morning to go lose himself in something he absolutely didn't want. And he was going to leave because the one thing he knew for certain was that Becky Billings deserved something way better than Harry Slater.

"Go back to your friends," he whispered to her. "I'll be fine."

"Hot bath," was all she said. Then she leaned in and raised up on her toes. He could see by a brief wince that the motion was hurting her bad knee, but she didn't withdraw.

Not wanting to sully her, he didn't reach out to drag her against him and hold on tight against the storm he could feel coming. Instead, they traded a soft and gentle kiss before he turned and splatted his way up the rough stairs.

Harry climbed into the tub and sat down in it still fully clothed. He cranked open the faucets and tried to ignore the slowly rising murmur of voices below.

The sooner he was gone, the better off she'd be.

The shakes came on as the water rose past his ankles and he couldn't seem to make them stop.

# # #

Becky returned to the couch, favoring her bad leg. That last move of raising up on her toes had almost driven her back to trying to hop again. But he'd looked so hurt and lost that she would do it again.

She made it back to the couch and Jessica helped her get resettled. Tiffany regathered her knitting from where she'd dumped it on the floor and handed it over. Becky focused on getting restarted. One of the drawbacks to eyelash yarn was that it was so busy that it was almost impossible to tell whether or not you'd dropped a stitch. She carefully checked the main ply and welcomed the familiar rhythm once she could restart her knitting.

The conversation slowly resumed around her, a soft wash of friendly voices as pleasant as the rain on the barn's tin roof.

She'd had her fair share of lovers. Some were after just the sex, others willing to give more. A few had lasted a single evening, one had lasted a year before she'd realized that the sex was good, but there wasn't much else there for either of them. Even Greg, when he'd first returned to town three years ago, had been sweet. Neither of them knew it back then, but his high school crush on Jessica hadn't gone away and it had been enough to ultimately send them on their separate ways.

And in all that time, Becky tried to think of the most romantic moment any time in her history. The slow dance at Jessica's wedding had been incredible. The moment when Harry had swept a broken garden gnome into his arms and carried a princess upstairs to bathe and bed her had been completely swoon-worthy.

She looked up at the faces of her friends.

Gina's booming laugh spilled like an ocean wave, brightening multiple conversations. Peggy's late arrival was greeted with waves and catcalls of just what man had she been busy with that she was so late; a question she declined to answer with even one of her sharp comebacks. Tiffany, in her silent way, watching everything with a soft smile and missing nothing.

The most romantic moment in her entire life?

When a beautiful, sodden, grimy, frustrated man had come home to her, and then kissed her in front of her closest friends as if it was the most normal thing in the world.

What had Jessica's advice been?

"We just have to make sure that he figures it out."

Apparently he had. But there was still the old joke: a garden gnome could love a lawyer, but where could they live together?

Having no good answer, she let the conversation swirl around her without jumping in as she normally would.

Becky waited a long time, hoping that Harry would come back down to join her. She could understand why he didn't with all of the women gathered here. But that didn't stop her wishing that he would.

# Chapter 7

*It had taken a* lot of hot water before Harry's hands worked well enough for him to strip off his clothes. He'd squeezed them out as well as he could while sitting chest deep in the tub before dumping the sodden mass onto the bathmat.

When the shivers finally stopped, and the water was brown with the mud that had sluiced off him, he'd dried himself off and crawled into Becky's bed.

He could hear the laughter downstairs. He tried to pick out Becky's laugh, but couldn't. Another sign, as if he needed one, that something was wrong. If you couldn't recognize the laugh of the woman you were having sex with…that had to mean… something. Though he'd be damned if he knew what.

What a group of friends Becky had. A dozen people gathered together from different walks of life by a common interest: a brewer, a real estate agent, a teacher, a B&B owner, the owner of a movie house, and others. Did he even know a dozen people outside of his office and his clients? Because clients certainly didn't count as friends. He'd guess that the waiters and bartenders at his favorite restaurants didn't count. Gina's big laugh boomed out again from below and others joined in, but he still couldn't pick out Becky's.

He pulled the covers over his head to block out the sound of cheerful conversation. It went on forever.

He kept thinking about New Orleans. In September and October the heavy summer rains were tapering off and the temperature was easing to where it was tolerable for even an Oregon boy. There were fall film festivals, the three-day utter-culinary-mayhem of the Annual Louisiana Seafood Festival. Hell, even the Southern Decadence was a hoot to watch. Called the "Gay Mardi Gras," it made one hell of a party. Sure, he'd get his butt pinched, but hordes of straight women showed up for the festivities as well.

Instead, he was cowering under the bedcovers in an Oregon hayloft.

*Sure, like New Orleans is so great.*

He wasn't sure where that voice had come from, but he didn't like it much. He tried to think if he'd actually gone to a single festival in the last year and couldn't come up with one.

Instead his life was bounded by the cool silence of his air-conditioned condo, quiet restaurant meals mostly eaten alone, and the frantic pulse beat of the law offices. Yet another contractor looking for ways to force through a million-dollar change order on a client because they'd low-balled their cost estimate to get the job, and now needed to make it up in other ways. Yet another class-action lawsuit for criminal negligence in an oil spill that was soaking into the water table. Yet another massive embezzlement case at one of the casinos. Yet another CEO fighting molestation charges that were probably only too true but they were such a major corporate client that a personal criminal defense had to be mounted.

How many people had he defended that he'd rather see raked over Satan's coals for a few millennia?

Too many.

But that was part of being a lawyer.

Didn't mean he had to like it, though he loved the *challenge* of it. The law was interesting. It was a living, organic body of knowledge that was a blending of intent versus word of the law. There was a visceral joy in unraveling how case law and precedent affected the legal code. But it was the courtroom that he found most fascinating. Many thought courtrooms were impersonal, but his greats victories had been because he understood just how personal they were for plaintiff, defendant, jury, judge, opposing counsel, witnesses, and even the onlookers.

But he wasn't feeling terribly inspired by the whole mess at the moment.

He curled deeper into the flannel pillow and sheets, decorated with little beer steins, that smelled of the nearby ocean and the most amazing woman he'd ever bedded.

One he was going to hurt more than any woman he'd ever been with.

# # #

Peggy hung back as the others left, returning chairs to where they belonged and collecting cream soda empties.

Becky lined up the empties in the washer racks that would strip the labels and sterilize the bottles for the next usage. She really should go upstairs, but she wasn't sure what she'd find. A part of her wondered if Harry would be dressed and packed, just awaiting the end of the knitting group to say goodbye. Some irrational part of her wondered if he'd gone out through the hayloft and down the back stairs. Even though she knew that he'd never do anything so cowardly, a part of her had to clamp back on the panic of that possibility.

She finally came to a halt by the mash tun. There was still a full pallet of barley that Harry had unloaded and stacked that should be processing now…but wasn't. She sat on the big, burlap bags and wished she could chop off her leg and replace it with a new one that wasn't throbbing. The over-the-counter pain killers were upstairs and it had been too long between doses. She hadn't thought to bring them down this morning because Harry always took care of such things for her. After thirty-two years of taking care of herself, she was turning into a totally dependent, lame, weakfish of a woman who—

"Enough with that look, Becky." Peggy sat down on the next barley bag over and wrapped an arm around her shoulders.

Becky huffed out a breath hard. Then another trying to clear the negative thought maelstrom out of her system.

"That's better," Peggy gave her a small shake. "Doc says you're doing a good job of staying off the knee. Do it for another week and everything will be back to normal."

Becky winced and managed not to look at the stairs.

"Men however," Peggy didn't need to be a mind reader to see her thoughts, "move at their own pace, unless we nudge them along."

"Is that what you do?"

"Some men need more nudging than others. The Slaters were never the quickest lot." Peggy was gazing intently at the empty mash tun.

"Is there something that *you* want to be telling *me?*" Though Becky didn't feel like she had much in the way of advise for anyone, especially not as cool and together a woman as Peggy.

Peggy actually startled before squinting at Becky for a long moment. "Just look at…what Jessica had to go through with Greg."

"That's an evasion, Peggy, and you know it. Jessica was the one who Greg had to nudge along."

"True, but Harry is…"

"Yeah," Becky admitted when Peggy didn't continue. She let herself look at the stairs this time and wondered what she'd find waiting for her. "He really, really is." Wonderful. Amazing. And completely not part of Eagle Cove.

Peggy squeezed Becky's shoulders again and then rose to her feet. "Best foot forward, Becky. That's the best we can do. We put our best foot forward and we hope. Actually…" Peggy stared off toward one of the barn walls for a long moment. "That's good advise, just might take it myself." Then with a final hug, Peggy was gone.

"Wait!" but she was too late. Whatever Peggy had evaded saying, she'd very neatly taken with her.

Becky climbed to her feet and grabbed her crutches. Well, at least there was no question about which was her best foot to put forward. So, she'd do that and hope for the best.

Becky managed to slowly navigate the steps with one crutch and a plate of leftovers. She almost lost them and herself down the stairs. She was glad that neither Peggy nor Harry was around to watch her struggle—they'd have been pissed. But she finally managed to reach the loft still intact and would count that as a triumph of the day.

Her best case scenario was to find Harry reading a book or watching a movie on his tablet, basically hiding from the clouds of estrogen that had been sweeping through the brewery. Instead she found a bathtub with dirt still smearing the drying bottom, a mangled pile of clothes that was worth more than her entire wardrobe, and a lump under the covers—hidden except for a small tuft of Harry's golden hair.

Romantic moment number fifty-six: beautiful, sweet man lying under the covers and waiting for her.

For her.

It was hard not to giggle in delight, though she'd striven to train herself out of giggling. What looked charming on tall blond women like Jessica, looked flat out childish on women of small stature.

She hobbled over, her crutch and brace clunking as she went.

No response from the bed; he must be asleep.

She set the platter on the nightstand, and stripped down to t-shirt and leg brace. She shed the big brace, but kept the underlying knee support in place. She wanted to lose it as well, it was the only part of her that had never touched Harry, but she also wanted to heal as fast as possible so that they could do so much more once she took it off.

A voice whispered in the back of her mind that the speed of her healing was going to be outstripped by his departure, but she chose to ignore it as she watched him sleeping.

He was here. In her bed. It was a good thing, better than anything else she'd imagined, and there just had to be some way to make it last.

Peggy was clearly cheering her on. And Jessica thought it was possible even if she didn't know how.

Becky figured that she could take that one of two ways. Either Jessica was so happy about marrying Greg that of course she'd wish it to be true for everyone around her. Or second, maybe there was some semi-mystical thing that married women knew when they looked at an unmarried couple. Somehow they could see that it was simply right and they really knew it just was going to work out fine.

Her inner voice whispered to be cautious, to protect her heart. Becky kicked it to the curb.

She decided to bank on the mystical power of married women, peeled her t-shirt, and slid under the covers. She snuggled up close behind the sleeping Harry. She was too short to be on the outside of the spoon, but she lay gently against his back and slid an arm over his ribs. She knew it wouldn't disturb him, he was a deep sleeper, but when he did wake up she wanted him to know that she was there beside him.

The moment her hand slid onto his chest, he clamped a hand over hers so fast that she gave a little squeal of surprise. He pressed it hard enough against his heart that she was half afraid she was hurting him.

He didn't uncurl from his near fetal position. He didn't turn to her. He just held her hand over his heart, never once easing up on the pressure.

Not knowing what else to do, she stroked his hair with her free hand, and whispered , "Shh. It'll be okay. It was just a hard day."

His hair was so clean and soft. It smelled of her own shampoo. She guessed that she was leaving imprints on Harry's life just as he was leaving them on hers.

"I built us a hell of a trap, didn't I?" When he finally spoke, his voice came out rough with anger and soft with resignation. Any lesser man would have denied it, or not spoken about it in the first place, but not her Harry.

*Her Harry.* Gods but that sounded glorious.

Becky smiled against his shoulder blade as she kissed it, "I think I might have helped with that one."

"I'm so sorry. So sorry," he gasped it out. With her hand on his heart, she could tell he wasn't crying, might not be able to. But he was really hurting.

She knew it was stupid and dangerous, but she couldn't help being happy about it.

She'd thought that she was the only one foolish enough to fall in love in this relationship. They'd been together from a Sunday night dance to this Friday evening. Five days. Just five amazing days.

"Falling hard," was such a cliché, yet she'd done it. And now, for the first time, she began to have a sliver of hope that the same thing had happened to Harry. It didn't mean that there was a future for them—she still couldn't see that—but it meant she wasn't alone as she dangled by this thin twist of yarn.

She could feel the pain coursing beneath her hand. More surely than she could feel when a brew had cooked enough just by the sense of it.

"I don't have any answers," he clamped even tighter onto her hand.

She kissed his shoulder blade again, "If it makes you feel any better about it, neither do I."

He choked a bitter laugh, "No, actually, that doesn't help."

"C'mon," she pulled at him to get him to roll over. He resisted. "Come on."

He was reluctant at first, but finally rolled.

"We're not going to talk about it right now," she kissed him lightly on the lips. It was miracle enough for tonight that this wasn't just some five-night stand to him.

She pulled his face down between her breasts and cradled him there. Not as she would a lover, but simply to comfort his aching soul. She slid both of her hands into his hair and propped her bad leg on his hip as they lay side by side.

He stayed there a long time with his arms wrapped around her. He let her hold him for what seemed like hours before they made love. And when they did, it was a slow, gentle, silent act in which they were both far kinder to one another than any time before.

# Chapter 8

*Rise and shine, Counselor."* A hand smacked down on his butt, jolting Harry awake. "I want pie."

"Pie?" His mumble was absorbed by the pillow he was face down in.

"Yes, pie. Up and at 'em!"

Becky. Definitely Becky. She began poking at his ribs. Probing until she found…

"Shit!"

He tried to roll away but he was snarled in the sheets and couldn't seem to escape her fingers.

"Damn it, woman!" His ticklish spot was very ticklish.

He made a grab for her, but she made good her escape.

Opening one eye, he surveyed the situation. Beautiful woman wearing clothes (damn it), one crutch, and an evil grin. She stood in a pool of sunlight that made her dark-blond hair shine.

"The court wants her pie and she wants it now."

Woman in sunlight. Sunlight? "Shit!" He twisted around to look at the clock, but became only more snarled in the sheets and quilt. He tumbled off the edge and hit the floor with a loud thump. "I'm late for the diner."

"It's Saturday. The Judge is closed Saturdays and Sundays, his anti-tourist policy."

"It's Saturday?" He'd been in Eagle Cove almost a full week? He should have his head examined.

"Does your father really strike such terror into the heart of a grown man?" Becky was a smart woman and was keeping enough distance that he couldn't drag her down onto the floor with him.

"No." *Absolutely.* "At least not when you ask it that way." *And completely.* "Does he make me feel like a freaked-out kid who just screwed up, again, every single time he looks at me? If you ask it that way then," he tried to shrug it off and clipped his shoulder on the base of the night stand hard enough to hurt. "Yeah."

"He's used to scare me too," Becky nodded, backing up another step to remain at a safe distance. "He is always so proper that it seems that all of us mere mortals could never live up to his standards. But not anymore."

She was mostly upside down from his point of view, but her answer appeared guileless.

"Well, not really," her smile gave her away.

"Knew it! Though he certainly seems to like Jessica a lot," the only person on the planet the Judge had ever hugged. Harry untangled himself from the covers and heaved them back onto the bed.

"Everybody likes Jessica."

"Whereas everyone flat out loves you."

"Bull!"

Becky had perched on a kitchen stool with her crutch planted like a "No Crossing" sign between her knees, so Harry headed over to brush his teeth and get dressed. Then he spotted the still sodden mass of clothes by the tub. He hung them over the shower curtain rail and wondered if they'd ever be useable again. Eagle Cove was being awfully hard on his wardrobe. The tub was a mess; he'd clean it up for her later.

As he brushed his teeth, he began poking through his duffle. He went for dry underwear, the Santorelli trousers, and his last Hugo Boss shirt.

"Seriously," he spit and rinsed, then began dressing. "What do you think yesterday was about? You should have seen Jessica bolt out the door of the diner when I told her you'd been hurt. Every one of those women came rushing here to take care of you."

"They came to knit. They were just being nice."

"Allow me to quote the court's earlier statement: Bull!" His Nikes were still a mess; he should have taken them into the tub with him to rinse them out. That only left him with the Allen Edmonds Oxfords that he'd brought for the wedding. At the rate he was going, he'd have to replace those as well after he got home.

He looked up to see that Becky was squinting at him.

"You didn't see that? Well, it was obvious to me." Habit had him reaching for a tie and jacket before he caught himself. "You could see it in their faces. Marjorie Winslow was ready to have me dragged out and beaten on your behalf at the least provocation. Of course she always was an absolute terror. Jessica had one of those dreamy looks as if—" And Harry wished that he could cut out his goddamn tongue. He couldn't turn to look at Becky, so instead he knelt down to retie his Oxfords.

"As if," she picked up in a whispery voice, "she hoped for us what she found with your brother."

"As if," he finally agreed. But Harry couldn't bring himself to look up.

She slid off the stool and thumped over until she stood close in front of him and he was forced to look up at her face.

He tried to read what was there, but with Becky he always had to ask. However his throat was too dry to form words at the moment.

"I hope for it to."

Harry couldn't even breathe.

"But it isn't what I expect. What I expect is…" And the tease was back in her voice, but he couldn't make sense of it in the middle of this conversation.

"What?"

"What I expect is for you to take me out for pie."

The laugh burst out of him. All the terror of last night about how he would hurt her and the impossibility of their situation laid out this morning just flew out of him like an Oregon Coast windstorm.

Becky Billings was the most amazing and startling woman anywhere. He knelt before her and pulled her tight against him, his arms around her fine butt and his face buried in her stomach. She stroked his hair and he could feel her grin even if he couldn't see it.

He jumped to his feet, kissed her lightly but resisted the urge to do more, then bowed deeply. "Come, my lady. Your chariot awaits and I shall chauffeur you wherever you wish to go."

"Well, the first thing I need is my other crutch from downstairs if I'm going to navigate the descent."

"You—" Harry bit down on his tongue. She'd come up the stairs with only one crutch?

"Why would you—" Then he remembered the cold meal they'd shared in the middle of the night by the moonlight streaming in through the skylight and windows. The empty plate still rested on the nightstand on her side of the bed. *Her side of the bed?* That meant that he had a side and—

"You crazy woman."

She shrugged but made no denial.

Rather than fetching the other crutch, he scooped her off her feet and enjoyed every second she clung to him as he carried her down the stairs.

# # #

Becky almost let him drive, just to save his shoes. But it was too silly. It was less than a hundred yards from the back door of her brewery to Peggy's airplane hangar, but it would be a half mile drive or more to reach the airport entrance and double back. The path was well-trodden—either she or Peggy tromped along it several times a week and at least once every Saturday morning—and it wasn't too muddy from yesterday's rain. The path ran through this corner of the broad field of hay. Her father had put a gate in the fence years ago. Becky still latched it every time out of happy memory of her father's cows who always thought the airport grass looked so much sweeter. Every chance they had, they broke out, much to the consternation of pilots trying to land on the grass and gravel strip.

The airport itself consisted of the main hangar that Peggy used and five others that were enough to hold the aircraft kept permanently in Eagle Cove. They huddled with their back walls toward the ocean storms and the front walls open like carports for airplanes. Only Peggy's had actual doors that slid across. The runway itself was freshly mown. A sun-faded windsock dangled limply from a high pole—not a breath of wind to disturb the day.

The air was cool and damp, washed clean by yesterday's rain. There was a magic to a sunny morning after a rain. It felt as if the whole world had been scrubbed until it shined.

"Why are we going to the airport?" Harry eyed the path with clear distaste.

"Peggy said there's a thing among private pilots. They're always looking for an excuse to go flying."

"Which has what to do with pie?" Harry began picking his way around puddles and soggy spots like they were populated by alligators.

Becky splashed ahead in her single rubber Wellington, though she did have to be careful to keep the tips of her crutches from sinking in too far and to not dip her sock-and-brace clad foot into any puddles. "They fly to some airports for their sandwich shops or superior burgers. Some runways are right along beaches or up near great hiking trails."

"So we're going flying?"

"Well, we can if you want to and Peggy has time, but I'd rather have pie."

She glanced over. Harry was so confused that he stepped right in a muddy spot then jumped into the tall wet hay as if he'd been bitten. Roland Greene who rented and worked this field for the hay had gotten most of the field harvested and stored before the rains came. His mower had broken down though and this one end of the field had gone unharvested. Unless there was an unusually dry two weeks very soon, this section would be knocked down by the weather and he'd just have to plow it under for the spring.

By the time Harry returned to the path, his trousers were soaked from the calves down. He was even cuter than she'd thought, which was pretty damned cute.

"On Saturday and Sunday mornings Peggy serves the best pie for like a dozen counties around. Fliers from all over come in for it."

As if to prove her point, a small plane buzzed above them before turning to line up on the runway. She pointed a crutch and Harry looked skyward, this time having enough sense to stop walking while he looked up from the path across the field.

They reached the big hangar. She led Harry through the people-sized door that simply said, "PIE. Saturday and Sunday while it lasts."

# # #

Harry stumbled while crossing the high threshold.

High windows let light into the big interior, but most of it was in shadow. A monstrous yellow biplane dominated the space. It had two open cockpit seats with tiny window cowlings and pointed it nose to the sky because its tail rested on a tiny rear wheel. The struts between the wings and the trim were painted a gloss black. Even in the shadows, it gleamed. The last time he'd seen it had been a dozen years ago when it was a stack of exposed frames, a mostly-intact fuselage, and pallets of metal parts. It now glistened.

Beyond it was parked a small helicopter that seated four or six and was painted in the same brilliant colors. Across the nose of each was painted "Naron's Goldfinch Air." Of course, her aircraft were the colors of the little birds.

On the far side of the hangar was parked a moderate-sized RV. It had its stabilizer pins down and he could see that full hookups had been run out to it. Peggy must live there. It was one of the cut-above brands, he'd seen enough go by as bankruptcy assets to know. It would be very comfortable inside.

The front corner closest by the door had broad and generous bay windows facing out onto the airfield.

He watched the high-winged, blue-and-white Cessna 174 that had buzzed by over their heads drop down onto the tarmac with an amateur's hard bounce before settling into a smooth roll. A couple of big picnic tables were tucked up close to the big bay windows.

"Quick," Becky called to him. "Pick your flavor before they all get here." Through the thin walls he could hear the plane pulling up to the hangar as well as car doors slamming nearby.

To the side of the door there was a counter filled with pre-cut pies all neatly labeled. Several apple-rhubarb and peach pies sat beneath a warming lamp. A cherry cobbler and five pumpkin pies sat on open glass shelves, and a glass-fronted refrigerator case held several lemon meringue and a chocolate-peanut butter with a crunch topping. Every pie had a server under the first piece, except for the apple-rhubarb which was missing several pieces already. In the refrigerator case there was also a line of whipped cream canisters, the good kind that restaurants used with nitrous, not the pre-packaged ones like at The Puffin Diner.

There was a stack of paper plates and plastic forks next to a jar that said, "Five dollars a slice. Whipped cream included. Must eat here."

Becky noticed where his attention had gone. "People used to buy whole pies and she'd run out in the first ten minutes."

"Smart lady." He shoved a twenty-dollar bill in the jar.

"She only asks for ten for both of us."

"I want my Becky to have two if she feels like it. If they're as good as they smell, I certainly am." He hadn't meant to add the possessive to her name.

Maybe she wouldn't notice.

Her brilliant smile was far too bright for a treat of two pieces of pie and showed that she had absolutely heard it.

He'd never been possessive about a woman in his life. *My Becky.* Well, if there was ever one to feel that way about, she was dishing up a slice of apple pie and another of pumpkin. He'd always had a weakness for lemon meringue, a pie Mom had been especially good at. He took a slice of that and would decide what else to try later.

He was carrying Becky's pieces, the pumpkin nearly lost in a mound of whipped cream, over to the table she had crutched to when the hangar door slammed open. Two guys in their forties stumbled through the door, "I'll be damned, Josh wasn't leading us on. That's a nice change."

Close behind them Cal Jr. walked in.

"Buddy!"

Harry barely had time to set down Becky's slices before Cal came over and wrapped him in a bear hug with a bone-bruising thump of greeting on the back.

"Hey Beck! Peggy got any of her rhubarb?"

"She sure does."

"And you're not having a slice? That is so wrongheaded, girl. Almost as goofy as shacking up with some sharpie N'Orleans lawyer type. So high and mighty he doesn't even remember who his drinking buddies are on Friday Poker Night."

Harry had completely forgotten. Cal had mentioned it back at the wedding, but as neither of them had expected him to still be in Eagle Cove, he'd hadn't bothered to pay it much attention. Besides, last night he'd been curled up in a fetal ball like—

"Totally my fault," Becky rescued him. She even said it with a grin as if there'd been nothing but wild sex.

"Lucky shit!" Harry managed to absorb some of the shock of Cal's next congratulatory buffet with a sag and twist. "Save me a seat."

The two fliers sat at another table as two more planes pulled up in front of the hangar.

Harry doubled back to the big urn of coffee and slipped two more dollars in the jar. Becky was a cream-and-sugar woman, easy to remember because she was so bright and sweet herself. He pulled himself up sharp for a moment. That was the kind of trick he always used to remember a date's preferences so that he looked more attentive than he actually was. Hell, after the first trial break he could tell you how every single juror drank their cuppa and he wouldn't forget. He didn't like using those kinds of games on Becky.

*You know how she likes her coffee. That's all that matters, Slater.*
And it was.

He arrived back at the table just a single step ahead of Cal which was all that secured his seat directly across from Becky. He'd thought of sitting beside her, but decided that the chance to play footsie and just look at her made sitting across a better choice.

Cal sat beside him rather than beside Becky. "Guy's gotta sit where he can be in the glow of a smile like that one. He's really lighting you up, Beck. Looks good on you."

"Feels good too, Cal. We have to find a girl for you."

Cal grimaced and took a forkful of the apple rhubarb. "Not a lot of girls who think a grown man who goes to bed at eight and gets up by four to bake bread is a whole lotta fun."

"But it's such gooood bread, Cal." She drew it out with enough sexual innuendo to have Harry's body heating up. She caught his reaction, fluttered her eyes closed and groaned in a way he'd learned was an indicator that he was doing something really right.

He could see Cal swallow hard and the two flyboys stop eating for a moment to look over and see just what was causing her to make that sound.

"Just like this is such gooood pie." Under the table she ran her good leg up the inside of Harry's.

Harry's pulse picked up another couple notches until Cal shoved his shoulder against Harry's hard enough that he'd have gone off the end of the bench if it wasn't up against the wall.

"Damn Beck, cut that out," Cal complained. "I'm a single guy for crying out loud, not even getting it regular like some lawyers."

"Shut up and eat your pie," Harry told him, then whispered, "Loser!" as he held his forefinger and thumb in an "L" against his forehead.

And that set the three of them laughing.

He'd missed Cal. Good friends like him didn't come along every day. He'd seen him half a dozen times in twice as many years and he felt like his brother more than, well, his brother. Nothing that wrong with Greg, but he and Cal had been close.

"So what you're saying is I gotta find a girl who loves me for my bread?"

"Hey, you think I'd have caught a lawyer without my beer?"

"It is damn good beer," Cal agreed. "Mighta had some of it last night."

Odd. Harry only now realized that he had yet to have a taste of it. Jessica had apparently served Becky's beer at the reception—which he'd carefully flown in too late for—but only champagne and cider for the wedding.

While he wasn't watching, Cal stole the last forkful of his lemon meringue.

"You need to make lemon meringue beer, Beck. Just stir in some of this pie and do whatever it is you do."

Harry laughed, but he could see Becky go thoughtful.

"It would have to be a lighter beer."

He should know by now that brewing was the one subject she never joked about.

"A pale ale, like an IPA," Cal suggested.

"A lager," a deep voice declared like law from the end of the table. The Judge stood there holding a piece of the lemon meringue. "Anything heavier would overwhelm the subtlety of Peggy's pie. As good as your ma's," he pointed a plastic fork at Harry's chest. "May I?" he nodded toward the seat beside Becky.

"Please," she patted it for him to sit beside her.

Just as Cal had been wanting in on facing a package as cute as Becky, now Harry was faced with his father and wanted nothing to do with it.

"How's the leg doing, Becky?"

"Good as can be, sir. Your son's been taking good care of me."

Cal turned to waggle his eyebrows meaningfully at Harry.

"He'll never be a great brewer, doesn't have the passion for it, but he's been a very handy assistant."

Cal knocked his knee sideways into Harry's.

Harry knocked his knee back against Cal's.

Then Becky kicked him sharply in the shin with her Wellington—hard enough to make him yelp—at the same moment she was smiling up at the Judge. A glance down showed a big muddy boot print on the leg of his last clean slacks. And he wouldn't be surprised if a blood stain formed there in a moment. She'd kicked him hard.

# # #

Harry might be a successful lawyer and an incredible lover, but there was still a major dweeb in the mix. It really was like watching the two high school stars of the Pufflings soccer team fooling around in the back of the classroom rather than paying attention. And between them they'd just banged her bad leg hard enough to hurt.

Unlike Harry and Cal, who sat with their backs to the hangar, she'd seen the Judge's approach. She'd almost missed it, as he'd circled around behind the aircraft, but he could only have come from Peggy's RV. Which also explained why Peggy had avoided answering the tease about her late arrival to knitting yesterday afternoon. *What man had she been busy with that she was so late?* Gina's barb had hit dead center even if no one knew it. It seems that Peggy had taken her own advice after knitting last night.

*The Slaters were never the quickest lot.* Now Peggy's comment made perfect sense.

Becky wondered what that bit of information would do to Harry's presently adolescent brain. But if Judge Slater wanted to be discreet, she wasn't going to spoil it for him.

Peggy came out of the RV with a loose-hipped saunter that Becky would absolutely be doing if it weren't for the crutches and leg brace. At the moment Becky knew she was about as sexy as a forklift, but Harry wasn't complaining so she shouldn't be either. A couple of the fliers stopped Peggy at the Stearman biplane. They were obviously geeking out over the restoration. It was just as well because the Judge's reaction was as plain as day.

His attention hadn't just drifted to Peggy, it had zeroed in, and one of his quiet smiles eased the lines on his face. Thankfully neither of the boys noticed.

Becky rested her hand on the Judge's arm to distract him. It took him a moment to shake off his thoughts and turn to her. Now that he had, she didn't know what to say.

"Are you looking forward to being a grandfather?" It was the first and dumbest thing to come into her head.

The Judge's look acknowledged that without having to say aloud, "Is there anything that *you* want to be telling me, young lady?"

Then he smiled softly as if setting the question aside.

"As I consider it, I find the thought to be rather new. I am deeply sorry that my wife didn't live to see how happy they are."

"You can be happy for them too, Dad," Harry's voice was harsh.

Becky spun to look at him.

Harry's face had taken on a grim set. The Judge merely looked sad. She'd seen that anger before between son and father, but hadn't seen it so blatantly displayed.

Becky shot for another subject change, "Will you be ready for Salmon Days?"

"I do not understand why I must open on the weekend for tourists," the Judge looked relieved at the subject change. "But my daughter-in-law insists and I agreed to follow her guidance in order to promote Eagle Cove."

"Salmon Days?" Harry's look slowly shifted from aggressive to puzzled. A good change.

"Pay attention, dude!" Then Cal smacked him on the back of the head.

Harry's expression shifted to a different kind of irritation—now aimed playfully at Cal instead of at his father with a load of anger. Thank goodness.

Cal continued as if Harry's attitude was utterly meaningless to a man of his size. "Your sister-in-law is a marketing genius. Why do you think the town is so busy? She did a whole number on the snowbirds using September to travel down the coast toward their winter homes. The campground is solid with RVs and the hotels are mostly full even though tourists have to go out of their way and cross a pass to reach us from Highway 101. Next weekend is the first weekend in October, time for the big Fall celebration: Salmon Days."

"And we," Becky held up a palm to Cal who smacked it with a high five, "are going to kick ass!" She got a high five out of the Judge as well which surprised her and apparently shocked his son.

"Doing what?"

"Beer tastings!" Becky called out. "And a beer garden at events."

"Amazing baked goods!" Cal declared.

"Feeding tourists breakfast on the weekend," the Judge's tone was dead dry but his smile gave him away.

"Airplane and helicopter rides!" Peggy sat down next to Cal, playing it a little coy by sitting opposite the Judge. Becky half wondered if they'd soon be playing footsie under the table, though it was hard to imagine the Judge doing something like that. Then Peggy smiled over at her in a way that said the Judge might not have a choice on whether or not that happened.

"Greg is doing his gourmet thing," Becky started ticking off on her fingers. "Salmon Fishing Derby for the biggest fish, the youngest and oldest fisherman to make a catch, and a couple of other things. Wood chopping contests with a raffle to benefit community hall projects, not to mention firewood for the town's old folks. Sunday we have a chainsaw art demonstration that is drawing carvers from all up and down the coast—they each get an eight foot section from Saturday's Jack and Jill handsaw event. We have a couple boats coming down from Depoe Bay for the weekend to do gray whale spotting tours during their winter migration south. The whole town is really doing it up."

"Huh," was Harry's thoughtful input.

Actually, *Huh!* was appropriate for her, too. She'd only cooked a single batch of beer, and too many things had gone by the boards this week. Next week was going to be a hard push to get ready.

Time for play was almost over.

It hit her like a punch to the chest. She tried not to look at Harry, not directly, but time for play *was* over. Or near enough. By Monday she'd have to be in full scramble mode no matter what shape her knee was in.

Maybe, if she was careful and didn't mind not sleeping much, she could carve out the rest of the weekend with Harry, but their fling really was coming to an end.

It ripped at her heart, but being a practical girl, she'd have to face that.

Really soon.

But not quite yet.

# Chapter 9

*Harry spent the day* doing his best to make everything perfect.

He took Becky for a drive along the coast. They had a chilly picnic at the stone gazebo perched high on the cliffs above Yachats. They drove up the Alsea River just because Route 34 along the valley was so beautiful in the fall where it wandered through the Siuslaw Forest.

At the Alsea Mercantile, the only real store in the town of a hundred-and-sixty, they worked on naming the twelve-point Roosevelt elk whose head was mounted above the front door along with a display of old saws and rifles. They bought a pint of Tillamook Caramel Toffee Crunch ice cream and wandered up and down the hardware aisles making up purposes for bizarre pipe fittings.

He took turns feeding himself and Becky by the spoonful as she still had her crutches. The game was a little spoiled because Becky knew everything about almost anything hardware, whereas he was stumped by even the simplest item.

"I'm a lawyer, not a brewer, so sue me," he grumbled at one point. He wasn't used to environments where he knew less than anyone else in the room.

"Deal. Can I hire you to sue yourself?"

"Sure." The way he was feeling, he might sue himself just on general principle.

"Good, come here." They were somewhere between sump pumps and engine cleaners that smelled as sharply oily as the water had when he'd had to personally visit the site of a coastal spill. She pulled him down into a sloppy, sweet, caramel-flavored kiss that had him curling his toes it was so good. He cursed that his hands were filled with ice cream and spoon so that he couldn't take more advantage of the moment before she broke it off.

"What was that for?"

"Down payment. Consider yourself hired. Defendant is one Harry Slater. Go get him, Counselor!"

"How do *you* do that?"

"What?" She crutched off into ducting and air conditioning. How did anyone sell air conditioning in coastal Oregon?

"The legal talk thing."

Becky did one of her cute-as-hell blushes, "Dylan McDermott in *The Practice*. Total dreamboat during my lonely teen years. I own the complete set, all eight seasons. How do you do it?"

"Do what?"

"The legal thing."

"By shutting off my heart."

She stuttered to a stop in switches and turned to face him. This aisle smelled vaguely of burnt rubber. Or bad electrical smells. Carbon arcing or some such.

His spontaneous answer lay there between them on the scuffed cement floor mud-tracked to a dull brown. Harry closed his eyes. He so didn't want to face this. He enjoyed his job and he was damn good at it. Honestly he did, especially as long as he kept telling himself that.

"Ehhhh!" Becky made a harsh, penalty-buzzer noise. "Try again, Counselor. This girl knows better. Frankly, if I was you, I'd sue the dude who said that. Now give me another bite of ice cream. I think you've been hogging it."

He dipped in the plastic spoon and fed her another bite.

"Yum!" Then she turned and continued their slow pace along the aisle, leading him away from the site of his vomiting out his darkest secret. It *was* how he got through so many cases. *Focus on the law. Precedent, code, procedural errors. Ignore the facts because attorney-client privilege protects the client no matter how much you know them to be guilty.* How many times had he held proof of fraud in his hands and tried to figure out a way to be sure that opposing counsel didn't know it existed but without, quite, breaking the rules of discovery? Probably about the same number of times as opposing counsel had done the same.

Becky Billings had just told him he still had a heart, and then made no big deal out of it.

All the way back down to the coast and out to Eagle Cove he tried to juggle the facets of the situation, but they weren't coming together. Normally he was the one who could take the turbulent mass of evidence, testimony, and the law and find a way to create a coherent presentation that an everyman jury could follow and at least think they understood.

How he and Becky Billings could possibly fit together was not one of those situations.

By the time they arrived back at the brewery, there was just time to clean up and go to their fancy dinner. He was thankful that there was something to occupy them.

He dressed in the suit he'd worn to Greg's wedding, and felt moderately ridiculous, but it was either that or beige wool gabardine on which you could still see the outline of a Wellington boot print.

Harry half hoped that Becky would opt once more for the little black dress, even if the evening was chilly for that. He really would enjoy taking it back off her later tonight.

Instead, she dressed in a black satin blouse and form-hugging slacks that made her legs look long and her hips look almost as sexy as he knew they were. She only wore the lighter brace, which had disappeared under the slacks. She accented the outfit with…

Harry laughed. He couldn't help himself, it was just knocked out of him.

Becky wore his missing Oregon Ducks silk tie. The greens and golds somehow drew out the color of her eyes, her lips, and her hair. She wore it like a loose cravat before it disappeared into the blouse. It was only too easy to imagine the tie running out of sight down her cleavage.

"Inside or outside the bra?"

"*That* is a question that you'll have to solve later, Counselor, if you get lucky that is."

"Well, if my little brother cooks even half as well as everyone says, I have high hopes."

"He cooks better." Then Becky groaned with disgust as she picked up her crutches.

Harry hurried forward to get ahead of her going down the stairs in case she lost her balance and needed rescuing.

She didn't.

But she did look spectacular climbing into his car.

# # #

"I don't know how to do this." Harry held the car door for her, but Becky didn't climb out. She didn't know how to face her friends through a whole dinner at The Puffin. She didn't know how to sit across from Harry and not have every emotion in her heart splatter out for all to see.

"You release the seatbelt. Then you swing out one leg. After that—"

Her baleful glare apparently got the message across.

He squatted down so that they were eye to eye. Damn, he had to be a considerate guy on top of being kind. She couldn't find any anger against him. Against the circumstances that surrounded them? Easy! But not against Harry Slater.

"For days I've been looking forward to taking you to a fine dinner. The fact that it's made by my little brother," he made a grimace like he'd bitten a lemon, but he kept the tone light and funny and added a wry smile that made her want to kiss it so that she could be a part of that smile as well, "is an issue that can't be helped."

"Why?"

"Because dining out with a beautiful woman who I care so much about just sounds like a really good idea."

*Who I care so much about.* She studied his eyes and ignored the curious looks they were receiving from others walking along the sidewalk toward the diner. He did care about her; she knew that. So why did it keep surprising her? A man like Harry wasn't likely to use any stronger words. That seemed to be part of their unspoken agreement—she hadn't used the L-word either. Heaven help her though, she couldn't imagine ever loving another man the way she loved Harry Slater.

"So, I have an idea," he continued to balance easily in a squat she couldn't even do any more.

"Thank god."

"There are two legal terms I can think of to apply to this matter," again that melting smile of his, "should it so please the court."

It took an effort, but Becky pulled on the mental cloak of their game of her being the court and he the counselor.

"The first," Harry continued apparently oblivious to how hard this was, "is *de novo*. It means 'as if new.' An appellate review *de novo* is one made without consideration of the trial judge's ruling. The other is *pro tem* which is a fancy way to say 'only temporarily.' What if we declare tonight to be dinner *de novo pro tem?*"

Or maybe Harry did understand how hard this was. Maybe he too felt the pressure of the outside world that was squeezing in upon their idyll.

"Dining *de novo pro tem?*" She like the way that sounded. Dinner as if new, at least for the moment.

He nodded and held out his hand to assist her from the car. "Just us. Ignore the world."

"Just us," he took her hand and with that connection made, she could do nothing other than slide free of the car.

Unable to take her hand because of the damn crutches, he instead looped a hand about her elbow as they proceeded to The Puffin, climbed the steps, and went inside.

# # #

Becky's gasp of wonder almost pulled Harry out of their fragile bubble. It was as if he could see the edges crackle, and then ease back together.

The battered Puffin Diner had been transformed into The Puffin. Instead of bright fluorescents, twinkle lights were draped across the ceiling like stars. The Formica tables, so scuffed with age that they were almost colorless, had been lined up into two long communal-style tables and covered with tablecloths of midnight blue. Fat white candles set on crystal dishes cast small pools of light over shining silverware and pale blue linen napkins.

Harry ducked into the back room to grab a footstool to support Becky's leg, and helped her settle in the seat farthest from the service window and kitchen. For a moment he was afraid that some local would take the next set of seats along the table, but two out-of-town couples sat in the next four chairs. It was rapidly apparent that they were friends on their journey south, enjoying a fine meal before getting on the road again. They were as content to ignore he and Becky as they themselves were glad to be ignored.

He scooted one of the candles until it lit just their portion of the table and left a line of soft shadow between them and the rest of the long table. With the darkened window to their other side, they were almost alone in the entire restaurant except for their candle-warmed reflections.

"Haven't you been here for dinner?" Becky was looking around like a child gawking at a circus.

"Only in the beginning. Greg started out by inviting a few friends over to test dishes on. We'd all kick in ten bucks, except me, I'd kick in a case of beer. But since he took it upscale, it's out of my price range."

"Methinks the court is fibbing." Her tone definitely didn't ring true.

She fiddled with a salad fork but didn't answer.

"You came!" Greg blasted through the side of their little sanctuary. He was almost unrecognizable in his immaculate white chef's coat. He clasped Becky's hand in delight then turned to Harry, "Good job, bro. She's been very resistant. I'm gonna knock your socks off, Becky." He gave her hand a final squeeze and disappeared again.

"Now I know the court is fibbing."

Becky toyed with her fork some more, but finally answered. "Greg doesn't serve his meals with wine, he serves them exclusively with Billings beers. I used to come and do the 'beer talk' at the dinners, but as he got better and better, I felt more and more out of my league. I finally begged off."

Which Harry's courtroom sense told him was only half the story, so he waited.

"Well look," Becky finally looked up at his eyes, but gestured down the table.

He did and it only took a moment to see what she was talking about. There were a few family groups, but this was definitely a couples' restaurant. He'd run into those in New Orleans and learned the power of taking a date to one that felt like this, but she was right—he never ate in them alone.

"Point taken. But tonight is good, isn't it?" How pitiful was it that he was begging to have his ego stroked that he was doing this right?

And her radiant smile did exactly that. "It is, Harry. This is very good."

The first course arrived. Delicate sushi rolls of crab, salmon, and butternut squash. It seemed an odd combo until dipped into the spicy black bean sauce. It was paired with an ale so light and delicate that it was almost saki-like in its clarity and was served in tiny coffee cups.

"Yours?"

Becky nodded, then closed her eyes. He could practically see her comparing and cataloging flavor profiles.

"Need a notebook?"

Becky almost snorted the beer as she tried to cover her laugh.

"No. I think I'm fairly happy with this one. I'd like to find a few more floral notes, but I'd be afraid to ruin it."

"Rose petals," he teased her.

"No, but maybe dandelion."

"I forgot. You don't joke about brewing."

"Never," she sipped again at the tiny cup of beer. "What don't you ever joke about?"

"Well, by the very nature of my job I'm the butt of the largest segment of jokes ever told. But I've learned that there are certain topics not to ever joke about with others: money with corporate types, and guilt or innocence with the obviously guilty. Though that isn't a bad way to find out if your client actually is guilty when they're playing coy."

Becky's laugh was appreciative and the bubble of their little sanctuary grew stronger and more solid. When they were served the butternut squash soup with wild mushroom and pancetta tortellini and paired with Barn Door Red Ale, it barely impinged on their awareness. The nuttiness of the beer complemented the hint of walnut in the pasta.

He tipped his beer toward her to acknowledge it.

"What else?" Becky bowed her head briefly at his accolade. She had a real modesty about putting herself forward, but none about the amazing quality of her beer.

"Never joke with anyone about the fact that the increased idiocy of their case is only going to augment the exorbitant size of your fee—no matter that it's absolutely true."

Becky was the most willing of listeners.

"And never, ever, under any circumstances, joke about a woman's hair, clothes, or anything whatsoever to do with marriage."

Her expression froze despite the warm candlelight.

And if he could remove his foot from his mouth surgically he would do so.

He could see Becky dig in and struggle to bail him out of his own stupidity, but there was no helping him this time. He'd shattered the illusion and they were once again sitting in an old diner built in a ridiculously small coastal town. The buzz of conversation along the two tables only made the stark silence at their end all the more painful.

# # #

Becky hadn't let herself think that word. She'd built fortress walls around it every time she looked at Greg or Jessica and saw how insanely happy they were. It was fine for them, but she couldn't imagine it for the Becky Billings of the world. The bolt of raw envy knocked her speechless.

Harry had given her a glimpse of what was possible. It was no more than that, but it was like a tiny taste of a perfect beer, and then never again being permitted to have any.

But this dinner, this moment was so precious that she didn't want to mar it with her own issues. She scrambled around for a tease and felt a wave of relief when she finally found one.

"What's wrong with my hair?"

Harry's jaw simply dropped. He didn't laugh like he was supposed to, or struggle to backpedal which also would have been okay. He didn't even take the obvious opportunity to pay her a compliment. She had been too self-conscious with him in the room to spend much time fixing it up (another disadvantage to an open floor plan), but still she'd thought it looked nice brushed out over her shoulders with a simple copper barrette holding it back to one side.

Instead, he looked at her with such warmth that she could feel heat rising into her cheeks.

"You are, without contention, Becky, the most amazing woman ever."

She had to look down at the table and study her empty bowl. Between one eyeblink and the next, the bowl was slid away and a fillet of bright pink-orange salmon surrounded by crab-stuffed mushroom caps took its place. A light sauce of rice wine vinegar and dill was balanced by the tartar sauce built into the mushrooms.

The unexpected pairing of her sweet and malty Deep Ocean Bock was…incredible.

"This is how you make me feel," she forced herself to look back up at Harry.

"I do?" He inspected his dish with a puzzled frown.

"Yes, you do. You make me feel incredible enough that I can almost believe it."

"You should. You absolutely should."

The rest of the meal passed in soft tones and meaningless conversation.

And the rest of the night passed in soft tones and meaningful lovemaking that permanently changed the way she'd ever think of herself again.

# Chapter 10

*Harry woke early on* Monday. It was dark and the rain that had been a soft background to their Sunday had been replaced by a heavy drencher. It pounded down on the barn's tin roof and pinged off the glass of the skylight. Stiff gusts of wind slapped it against the seaward windows like a thousand ball bearings dumped on a sheet of steel.

He didn't need to reach out to know that he was alone in Becky's big bed; it felt different when she wasn't there.

Saturday night after the dinner, he'd kidnapped the stout white candle from the table. Becky had accused him of malfeasance aforethought and he hadn't denied the charge. But she'd also cooed with pleasure when he'd relit it in her hayloft apartment. He'd made love to her—there was no longer any way he could just call it sex—trying to outlast the slow-burning candle.

It was still burning when they finally slept curled tightly together.

Sunday they'd left the bed only for food and a shared bath in the big tub. They'd stretched out together and watched a half dozen episodes of *The Practice* on Becky's computer and he had to admit that with the attractive distractions of LisaGay Hamilton and Kelli Williams, the show wasn't that far off the mark.

At dusk, they'd relit the candle, but neither of them had been up for much, neither physically nor conversationally. Mostly they'd lain together and held on tightly.

And now, Monday, he'd woken alone. The candle had burned out and the only light was a soft glow coming up the stairs from the brewery.

He felt positively somnolent as he moved through the morning's actions: making the bed, brushing his teeth, getting dressed, packing his bag. It was as if someone else was performing the actions, especially the last.

Harry didn't want to go, but it was time.

*I get through it by shutting off my heart.*

So he did. Each piece of clothing held a memory. Ripped khakis from unloading her truck. A bleached spot on a dark blue Armani shirt where cleaning solution had splashed while he helped her scrub one of the tanks. The dried mud that had filled every little hole in his Allen Edmonds Oxfords. At least the Nikes were dry, mostly.

He barely managed to hold it together when he found the Oregon Ducks tie tucked into the pocket of his suit. He'd worn it to the wedding as a tease to his brother who had gone to culinary school rather than college, but it had become a real thing with Becky. It was the only clothing she'd worn for most of their stolen Sunday together. He zipped it into the suiter bag along with the Michael Kors gray two-piecer that he'd worn to that cozy dinner.

He'd been using the extra toothbrush that he'd found that first night while Becky had slept on the couch below. The decision on whether he should take it or leave it was nearly the final straw.

*I get through it by…*

Talk about a sucky mantra. Those things were supposed to be uplifting, weren't they?

He moved down the stairs quietly and set his bags by the door before going to find Becky. He located her deep in the brewery. She was leaning against the copper cooking kettle right where they'd taken each other like it was the best thing in the—

*I get through it…*

He stopped only a few feet away, but couldn't move closer.

She faced away from him. Her head hung down and her shoulders were shaking.

What was he supposed to say?

Should he take her in his arms? He half expected that she'd strike out at him if he did and he wouldn't blame her. But if he touched her, how was he ever supposed to let her go?

"Becky?" He could barely hear his own voice over the low hum of pumps and heaters.

But she heard it and flinched as if he'd slapped her.

He didn't know what to do or what to say. He caught himself shuffling from foot to foot, a habit that his first defeat during a law school mock trial had trained out of him. "Student projected a deep lack of confidence with body language, particularly with the constant shifting of weight from one side to the other."

She leaned her forehead against the kettle.

"I—"

"Just go!" Her shout blasted out. "Look, Harry. It's been wonderful, but now you need to just go." Her voice was ragged and thick with pain.

He took a step forward.

"Don't!"

He froze. And when she moaned he didn't know what else to do.

He turned and left the brewery. At the door he stopped for one last look around the living room. He could hear the echoes of her friends' laughter, could almost see the women who loved her.

They would take care of her. Some day she'd be glad that he'd gone. She deserved so much better.

He hated that thought, but didn't know what else to do. He took his bags and went.

# # #

Becky didn't hear him go, but she felt the pressure change as the front door opened and then closed again. A chill breeze slipped into the warm brewery and set her to shivering.

The silence was impossibly deep, far quieter than when her lover had been sleeping upstairs, even if she'd no longer been able to tolerate lying beside him.

She braced her hands against the cool copper kettle, so warm when the two of them had lain naked against it.

Enough. It was time to do what must be done.

As she tried to stand up straight, her knee twinged. It wasn't bad, but she didn't have the energy to overcome even the minor ache.

Instead she let herself fold down onto the cold concrete floor. There, she curled into a small ball and let herself weep.

Becky wept through pain and tears. She wept until her eyes were dry and her chest ached as if it had been crushed, and still she couldn't stop. She curled more tightly around the agony and it only hurt worse.

Dying would be less painful; it just had to be.

# # #

Harry parked at the back of The Puffin Diner.

He wasn't sure why he was here. Habit? To say goodbye? Something for the road? The rental's dashboard clock read 5:50. Time to go to work. No… But it was…

Having no better plan, he tugged the collar of his jacket more tightly around his neck, and hurried in through the back door.

The normalcy was comforting. The Judge at his grill, giving the immaculate surface a final scrub with a bronze wool pad. The familiar odor of the first pot of coffee on to brew.

"Hey, bro!" Greg swung by and punched him on the arm. "Come to lend a hand?"

"I guess." Not really.

"Could use some more silverware sets."

Harry didn't take off his jacket, but stepped out of the kitchen and over to the service station. He began taking a knife, fork, and spoon, rolling them in a paper napkin, and putting a sticky strip around them.

He made up sets until he ran out of forks and then stood there with no idea of what to do next.

Greg dumped a pile of plastic-covered menus at the service station.

Harry read down through the options until his eyes hit the wavy black line drawn through "Waffles (with blueberries when in season)."

"You'll need to reprint these," Harry marveled at how normal his voice sounded.

"Why?" Greg stopped hurrying around and was being so cheerful that Harry wanted to club him with the coffee pot.

"The waffles."

"What about them?"

"The waffle iron got fixed."

Greg grabbed his shoulder and twisted him around, "Say what?"

"The waffle iron. Peggy fixed it. What's the big deal?"

"Of course you wouldn't get it." Greg's hand clamped harder and harder on Harry's shoulder as he slowly turned to look through the service window at the Judge.

"Peggy *fixed* it?" Greg asked their father.

The Judge was watching them, but didn't say a word.

*Goddamn reticent asshole.* Harry couldn't find much heat to put behind the thought though. As a matter of fact, he couldn't find any emotion about anything.

Harry tried to shake off Greg's hand; it was hurting. He finally clubbed it aside hard enough to make Greg yelp.

"Ouch! Damn it, Harry!" Then Greg squinted at him. "You look like shit. What happened, Becky finally grab some common sense and dump your sorry ass?"

Harry's fist connected with Greg's chin hard enough to smash his brother against the counter. With a roar that ripped at his throat, Harry dove at his brother.

Greg's counterstrike hit hard enough to hurt, but not enough to slow him down. Silverware scattered to the floor. The pile of menus flopped over and spread out across the linoleum. They made the footing as slick as an ice skating rink.

Harry didn't care.

He pounded his fist into Greg's gut and earned a very satisfying grunt.

They fell.

His attempt to knee Greg in the balls caught him on the thigh.

Greg managed a grab onto Harry's jacket and used it to throw him against the line of stools bolted to the floor. The pain blew sparks into Harry's vision.

His little brother was almost clear when he managed to grab an ankle.

Greg lashed out with his other foot and caught Harry on the shoulder, but Harry didn't let go.

This time. Once and for all. He'd really—

Pain sliced through the red haze over his vision.

Someone had his ear and was yanking on it hard.

It hurt too much to even fight against.

He had a brief vision of a small woman with curly red hair dragged back in a ponytail.

Peggy…was hauling him toward the door by his ear.

Greg managed a brutal gut punch that cost Harry the last of his air, leaving him barely able to stumble where Peggy was dragging him.

"I've got the other one," a male voice boomed just as Peggy led Harry out onto the porch and over the railing. He tumbled head over heels to land flat on his back in a mud puddle.

A moment later a massive weight slammed into him as Cal Jr. dropped Greg over the porch rail and right on top of him.

Harry tried to groan, but didn't have enough air.

Greg managed a groan, but little more. He finally flopped off Harry until they were lying side by side in the puddle. The Puffin was exposed to the beach and the heavy rain was backed up by a lashing wind. It was like ice cold acupuncture against every bit of uncovered skin.

Harry shoved himself up to a sitting position and managed to lever himself against the stone foundation of the porch. From here the steps afforded a little protection from the slicing wind.

Greg forced himself around until he too was leaning against the porch with Harry.

Harry punched his arm. Greg punched him back. Neither of them were able to make much out of it.

"Who the hell bit your ass, Harry?"

"Why do you care so damn much about a fucking waffle iron?"

Greg slicked back his hair and then made a vain effort to wipe the rain off his face.

Harry didn't even bother trying. He was starting to feel where Greg had caught him. His ribs weren't going to be playing racquetball anytime soon.

"You say Peggy fixed it?"

"Sure, on Friday. Took her about ten minutes other than getting some parts."

"Shit! I could have done that. Hell, it was so easy, you could have done it."

Greg jostled his shoulder but Harry didn't care enough to do more than jostle him back.

"The waffle iron broke the same day that Ma died. Neither of us could face touching it."

"Can't believe the old man even noticed she was gone."

In moments Greg was straddled over him and had a fist pulling Harry's jacket collar choking tight. "You don't know shit, asshole. You didn't watch him cradle Ma in his lap for hour after hour, day after day. You didn't see him age twenty years the day she died. Why the hell do you think I stayed in Eagle Cove? At least at first it was because I couldn't bear the thought of him being alone." Greg shoved him hard against the foundation before flopping back into the mud to sit beside him. A gust blasted along Beach Way hard enough to make waves in their personal, private mud puddle.

Harry had always assumed that his father was just a cold son of a bitch. But he *had* aged. He remembered the change at the funeral. He'd almost walked past the Judge he'd been so changed. If Harry hadn't been so wrapped up in his own misery, maybe it would have meant more at the time.

"If he had fixed the waffle iron," Greg stared up into the rain, "Maybe it would mean that he'd finally accepted Ma's death or something. But that Peggy fixed it… I don't know."

"They're sleeping together," Harry knew it was true as soon as he'd said it. All of the little pieces fell into place. The way she'd rested a hand on the Judge's arm. Saturday morning getting pie, the Judge hadn't been there when Harry and Becky had arrived. But he also hadn't come in the door that Harry had been facing. That meant he had been in the RV with Peggy.

"No way!"

"Count on it, baby bro." His father had moved on and found another woman as if anyone could measure up to Ma. On top of that, he'd commercialized Ma's art, selling it on t-shirts, hats, posters, and all of that other tourist crap. He wasn't cherishing her memory no matter what his brother thought.

"Well," Greg wiped at his face again as the water continued to drip off his nose. "Ain't that something. So what's up with you and Becky anyway?"

There were some things that Harry didn't want to talk about.

He forced himself to his feet, ignored the charley horse where Greg had kneed his thigh. He patted his pockets. Good, he'd managed to keep the car keys.

He crossed to the far side of the puddle then stopped and turned to look down at Greg.

"That was a hell of a good meal, Greg. And you have an amazing wife. Take good care of her."

Then unable to face what he could never be to another amazing woman, Harry trudged around the diner to his rental car, climbed in, and drove out of Eagle Cove.

# Chapter 11

$H$*arry hit the discount* department store out by the Portland airport. He bought the first jeans he'd owned in a decade, a t-shirt that didn't have anything to do with the coast or Oregon at all, and a pair of cheap shoes that felt like they were trying to reshape his feet. The dressing room trash bin he filled with the Nikes and everything else he'd been wearing—it wasn't even worth the effort to see if any of it was salvageable.

He skipped Vegas and flew home on the first flight he could find.

Tuesday, he checked in at the office. After a couple of meetings, he was told to take the rest of the week off and enjoy himself. There was a complete laugh. He hadn't even slept since leaving Oregon except in fits and naps filled with ugly dreams.

Wednesday he walked into the local shop for strong coffee and beignets. He took his usual chair at one of the open tables crowded onto the sidewalk and tried to focus on reading the newspaper. He must have missed some interesting local cases, but he couldn't make his mind focus on the printed words.

All he could picture was the woman who wouldn't look at him as he left.

While he'd been in the air, his phone had picked up a voicemail—a vitriolic diatribe from Jessica. Apparently Greg had called her right after Harry left town and she'd rushed out to find Becky. He considered trying to call back, but there was nothing to explain.

Harry closed his eyes. If he could feel any worse…but it wasn't possible.

He opened his eyes as a big man lowered himself into the other chair of the small table.

"What the hell are you doing here?"

The Judge merely sighed.

Harry rubbed at his eyes, "Okay, not my best effort. But seriously, Dad, what the hell are you doing here? Who's cooking breakfast?"

"Gregory has that well in hand. Peggy is assisting him."

"Are you and she…" he didn't even know why he asked. "Sorry, none of my business."

"She's a remarkable woman, Harold. As remarkable as your mother, in different ways."

"Why? Does Peggy have something else you can display on tourist crap for money like Ma's art?"

Again the sigh from the Judge.

Harry was just about to lash out or maybe he should just storm off, but the Judge held up a hand as if calling for silence in the court.

Old habits died hard; Harry waited. He was barely aware of the tourists rushing by, always in such a hurry, already working up a sweat though it was still early morning. The locals stood out in their relaxed, easygoing pace, one that Harry had never been able to match. He would always be an outsider, just by how he walked.

"I do not sell your mother's artwork for the money, Harold."

"Then why?"

"Because I want others to see the wonderful things she did. Her art is done. It died with her and nothing new will ever be created by her. But I remember her so well from even the least brushstroke. I didn't want that to die with her. Even if others cannot appreciate what they see, I do with every single t-shirt or gift bag that comes through the diner."

Harry leaned back in the chair, almost tipped it over backwards. Would have if not for the big man seated close behind him. He apologized then turned back to his father.

It was the longest speech he'd ever heard Judge John Slater make except from the courtroom bench. As a kid he'd often gone to court during summer breaks to listen to the cases and hear his father administer justice—a memory he'd almost forgotten.

His father's explanation also meant that Greg was right, the Judge missed his wife. Surprisingly, he had a heart…which was more than Harry could claim.

"That still doesn't explain why you're in New Orleans."

The Judge took one of Harry's beignets and bit into it. He chewed a long time for such a soft pastry, then finally set it down and looked right at Harry.

"Do you love her?"

"Do I what!" It came out loudly enough to make the people seated nearest to them jump in their seats.

"Becky Billings. Do you love her?" The Judge was wholly unfazed.

The coldest-hearted man the planet was asking him if he loved… Shit!

Harry shoved away from the table, tossed his paper down on his chair, but didn't make it even a dozen paces down the sidewalk. People jostled and bumped against him as he stood there with his head down. Looking up at the sky didn't help either. It wasn't that brilliant rain-washed blue of the Oregon Coast. Nor the roiled gray of a storm sweeping through. It was the washed-out blue-gray of a city tinged with heat haze and too many people.

"Do you love her?" Harry asked the sky. *How the hell am I supposed to know?*

He trudged back to the Judge with all of the enthusiasm of a defendant approaching the bench for sentencing. It was almost as hard as walking away from Becky just two days ago in a land thousands of miles away.

He collapsed back into his seat, "Do I love her."

"That is the question under consideration," his father sounded so much like Becky that he was torn between laughter and tears.

"I really hurt her, didn't I?"

The Judge nodded. "Luckily, when they love us, women are a forgiving lot."

He couldn't even forgive himself for walking away from her. For getting so involved in the first place.

"Parrish, Merryfield, and Roland offered me a full partnership yesterday."

"Very respectable," the Judge nodded. "I always knew that you'd do well."

"No you didn't. You thought I was an arrogant prick who would crash and burn."

Impossibly, the Judge began to chuckle. "Well, I will admit that I certainly feared that to be the case."

"What changed your mind?"

"Two things," the Judge was suddenly serious.

"Which were?"

"One, the way you assisted me at the diner. An arrogant boy would have wished me luck and walked away, but instead you did your very best day after day."

"It was the right thing to do."

"It was," the Judge nodded in agreement. "But it was no less unexpected. The second was Becky."

"What about her?" Harry was surprised at how desperate he was for any word of her.

"She is one of the most sensible women of her generation. She has a generous heart that she gives freely, but only so far.

She gives to her friends more than friendship would normally call for. But for herself she gives nothing…until she met you."

Harry slouched lower in his chair. "If you're trying to make me feel any worse, you're succeeding."

The Judge picked up his beignet and took another bite. He looked about at the pedestrians and the thick traffic along the street.

Harry in turn looked at the Judge and wondered that he was here. Yet it wouldn't be hard to find Harry, he was a creature of habit and a call to his secretary would reveal where to find him at this hour each morning. If there was any doubt, she could always access his phone locator software. He'd given her access because he was always losing the damn thing. But that the Judge had come all the way to New Orleans. There was more than just local-girl-made-sad-by-big-city-lawyer going on here. He really cared about Becky. And by extrapolation, maybe he cared about his eldest—

There was a train of thought about to jump off the track.

"Partner at Parrish, Merryfield, and Roland is quite an achievement," his father only ever repeated himself as a point of emphasis.

"I'm so glad you approve," Harry couldn't keep the sarcasm out of his tone. He knew it was a big deal without being told by the ever so popular, elected-to-six-terms-with-no-one-daring-to-run-against-him Judge Slater. PMR never recruited below top three and only from the best schools. Only one in twenty associates made partner.

"Have you accepted yet?"

"Have I—" Well, he hadn't actually. Not in so many words. He'd thanked them when they took him out to lunch at the club yesterday, but he hadn't actually said yes. "Why? Do you have a better idea?"

The Judge laced his fingers together as he always did when delivering a verdict, whether from the bench or at the dinner table. This time he kept his two forefingers pointed outward and tapped the tips together as he only did when he was uncertain of his choice of words.

"Just spit it out, Dad."

He grimaced, but stopped with the damned finger tapping. "There is an upcoming election for the 17th District Circuit Court in Newport, Oregon. There is a certain gentleman who is running uncontested for my old seat who is…"

"An incompetent boob?" Harry offered into the Judge's silence. His father had notoriously little patience for weak judges.

"An ambulance chaser has more savvy."

"It's way past time to file even if I wanted to be on the ballot."

"And yet you have retained your membership in the Oregon State Bar." An easy fact for the Judge to look up. It simply surprised Harry that his father had cared enough to do so. Yet he'd cared enough to travel all the way to New Orleans.

"Fought too hard to earn, just to let it go."

"You are a sensible man." The Judge managed to say it without sounding too condescending.

"And you'd suggest that I do this how?" He was actually rather flattered that his father would suggest Harry run for his old seat. Actually, it was tempting. Perhaps even very tempting.

The Judge slipped a large envelope across the table.

Harry opened it and half expected a snake to jump out at him.

Instead there was a campaign sign. Eye-catching. Sharp design.

*Vote Slater for Judge (Write it in!)*

"Your sister-in-law's work," the Judge nodded approvingly.

"But she hates me. Told me so at length on the phone." However, it was a chance to help dispense justice rather than spending his life trying to trick it. It would be a hell of a cut in pay, but he lived the high life now and it had done less for him than… Than a week with Becky Billings.

"Yes, Jessica is a passionate woman." The Judge pulled out his phone, dialed a number, and handed it to Harry while it was still ringing.

Oh crap!

"Hi, Jessica!" Harry tried to put on a cheery tone, then winced in preparation for the reply.

"Asshole! Nataly and I still want to cut your balls off!"

"I'd rather you didn't."

Jessica huffed at him over the phone. "But if you love Becky—"

"I do!" And the statement shocked him into silence but didn't slow Jessica down for a second.

"I know that, asshole brother-in-law, I'm just glad that you finally do. Okay, here's the plan that I have put together so far." And Jessica began rattling off promotions, ads campaigns, appearances at grange halls and Kiwanis meetings, and more that he couldn't even begin to follow. "You're kicking off your campaign on Sunday at Salmon Days, so you'd better get your ass back here by then." As if his compliance was a foregone conclusion.

And Jessica was gone.

Harry slowly handed the phone back to his father.

"That is a very determined woman."

"She is," the Judge agreed.

"I like that in a woman," because he'd never met a more determined woman than Becky Billings.

"So do I," his father nodded, obviously talking about the new woman in his life.

Oddly, for once, Harry didn't need to prepare a thing to make his decision. The jury didn't even have to leave the room for him to know his own verdict.

# Chapter 12

*Becky knew something was* up. But she didn't have time to think about what it might be. This week had been both wonderful and horrid beyond imagining.

Among the worst moments was that she'd been able to overhear what Jessica had yelled to poor Harry's voicemail over the phone. She loved her friend, and appreciated her staunch heartfelt support, but Harry had done nothing to deserve it. He had promised nothing and in so many ways given her everything.

All of the good things this week had kept her too busy to hurt for long.

After a few calls around, she'd hired Alex away from Cal Jr. "Let's hope he makes a better brewer than he did a baker," had been Cal's gruff statement after practically forcing Alex on her with high recommendations. The 5B Brewery had finally grown beyond anything she could manage herself. Alex drove deliveries, picked up product, and helped her with the heavy hauling work around the brewery. He seemed genuinely excited by the process. But even with his help, it had been a miracle that she'd been ready for Salmon Days at Eagle Cove.

The tasting room had been swamped, and not just with tourists. Four different pubs and three restaurants over in The Valley had come in for a tasting and left her with their cards to contact them about standing orders after Salmon Days was over. Peggy would have normally pitched in to help, but she'd been assisting Greg over at The Puffin Diner for most of the week. And now that it was the weekend, she had flights booked for almost every minute of daylight.

Becky had managed to corner her friend briefly over pie this morning, but Peggy had been very close-mouthed about why the Judge was out of town, suspiciously so. However, she had been completely open about how she and the Judge had hooked up. Becky had just assumed it was Peggy's doing, but couldn't be more wrong.

He'd come out to the airport one day over a month ago, with no one the wiser, and asked for a plane flight. He'd brought a picnic lunch and they'd landed on the sand of a remote cove.

It was hard to picture the Judge wooing a woman, but it sounded as if he'd done an excellent job of it, plying her with Becky's non-alcoholic cider, and homemade crab sandwiches.

"He spent a whole month courting me. It was only after I spoke to you on last Friday," she had the decency to offer a sympathetic squeeze of Becky's hand, "that I realized he was waiting for me to take the final initiative. 'Woman's prerogative,' was all he said when I asked. He doesn't say much, but the way he says it…" Peggy had looked very pleased with the results. "He was a little flustered that you caught on. You're the one who outed us."

"But I didn't tell a soul."

"No, but you proved to him that secrecy was not so crucial. He's not demonstrative, except in private, though he's very demonstrative there."

Becky offered the best smile she had, and struggled not to think of Harry. He too had been demonstrative and he hadn't been shy about being seen with her in public. Except now he was back in New Orleans.

The Saturday afternoon crowd had cleared out all the cases of two flavors entirely. She was trying to calculate if she had time to run a couple of batches through the bottler when Jessica and Natalya dropped by.

"Natya! I didn't know you were back in town for this."

"Just managed to get in. How's the knee?"

"Doc says that I was so good about wearing the big brace that I can probably lose it permanently Monday. Then I've got six weeks of physical therapy, but I should be good. I hate to ask this, but can you finish up here in the tasting room? I've got to get some bottling done."

Jessica and Natalya didn't even hesitate, they both jumped right in and shooed her off.

She came up behind each one and hugged them hard for a moment, "I love you both so much."

"Likewise, champ. Now go!"

Becky hurried back into the brewery and after about twenty minutes had the bottler running her Rushing River Stout into dark brown glass with her trademark bluebird-colored caps.

There was a clack and rattle as the bottles were jostled into position, filled under pressure, and capped. The labeler made a smooth slick sound and she taught Zander how to slide them into cases.

Peggy and Greg showed up while she was checking the progress of the next batch in the malt tun.

"Aren't you guys busy?"

"Dinner at The Puffin isn't for a couple of hours. I'm taking a quick break, thought I'd come out and see my wife."

Peggy just drifted over and started inspecting the gauges on the CCV tanks. The two of them often geeked together over plane engines and the brewing process. She soon had a wrench and was tightening fittings on the whirlpool filter that Becky had been meaning to get to all week.

Peggy made her feel calmer just by being here.

Tiffany wandered in, which was unheard of on a Saturday. In her typically odd way, she simply sat on the couch and without a word pulled out her knitting. Even though it was Saturday rather than Friday, others soon joined her: Gina, Marjorie…

Becky didn't have a moment to go over and ask what the heck was going on, not with the bottler running. The machine was awfully fussy and had to be watched over like a hawk to keep it running smoothly. She started teaching Alex the tricks to making it behave.

Jessica came in the back, "Crowd is thinning in the tasting room. Natya's shooing the last ones out the door."

"Thank god!" Becky loved the income she'd just received. She'd probably banked the next month of Zander's salary just from the sales that the tasting room had generated, but she really needed for everything to just slow down for a moment. Tomorrow was going to be even crazier.

"Someone just handed me this," Natalya came in and shoved an envelope into Becky's hands.

There was no address or marking.

She started to pull it out and swore. It was a legal document with the line numbers down the side and the header block of a lawsuit title.

"I don't have time for this."

She tossed it aside, but Jessica retrieved it and shoved it back into her hands.

Becky pulled it out from the envelope and began reading.

"Pleading for Forgiveness," she read aloud. "What the hell?"

"Keep going," Peggy prompted, suddenly at her elbow.

"The party of the first part, hereinafter named Harold Davis Slater…" Becky lost her breath and leaned back against the copper cooking kettle. It was warm. She'd started heating it earlier so that it would be up to temperature as soon as the mash was ready for cooking.

Natalya snatched the document from her nerveless fingers and continued reading aloud, "…hereby petitions the party of the second part, hereinafter named Becky Billings—fool doesn't even know that you're really Rebecca—for consideration of this motion being placed before the court."

Becky would have slid to the floor if she hadn't been wearing the big leg brace which kept her pinned upright with her back against the kettle.

"Do you want me to keep going?"

"Yes!" About half the people shouted, which was good, because Becky couldn't seem to catch her breath. The brewery felt so full with her friends all about her.

"How about if I finish it?" The Judge's deep voice sounded from the back of the crowd that had gathered. He moved up to stand beside Peggy.

"No," Harry stepped around him. "Let me."

Becky couldn't move, she couldn't breathe. She could only watch as Harry stepped into the brewery.

"It has been pointed out during a long drive across the country," Harry scowled at his father, but Becky could see there was humor behind it. "That counsel is not the sharpest lawyer there is. That title obviously goes to Dylan McDermott."

Becky almost choked herself on a half laugh.

Harry kept coming. Other than the bottler rattling away in the background, the room was dead silent.

"But he begs the court to consider the changed circumstances."

"What—" Becky had to cough to clear her throat. "What changed circumstances?"

"First," Harry came to a stop and took her hands. He held them tightly, rubbing his thumbs over her knuckles.

Even that simple gesture sent shivers up her spine. Really good shivers filled with hope.

"I appear to be the hot write-in candidate for the 17th District Circuit Court."

"Which is where?"

Harry smiled down at her, "Which is here. Newport anyway, but very commutable as my father proved for years."

Becky couldn't even breathe so it was a good thing that Harry continued without prompting.

"Second," and he kept her hands in his as he knelt so that she was the one looking down at him. "In front of these good friends and this copper kettle, I wish to state that I love you."

She could feel the tears running. They were the kind of tears with which a beer should be flavored. It gave her a recipe idea for a new brew that she'd think about later.

"Please, Becky Billings, please tell me that you'll have me, for without you, I'm lost."

Becky leaned back against the kettle, letting the warmth radiate through her and chase away the chill that had sunk into her body all week and threatened to freeze her heart forever.

"The court has a condition, Counselor."

He smiled up at her, "Name it. Anything."

And Becky knew that was true.

"The court demands," and she brushed a hand through his hair, before cupping his cheek and coaxing him back to his feet.

"The court demands that you kiss her here and now to prove your intent."

And Harry pressed her back against the warm copper and kissed her as the room erupted with cheers and applause.

# About the Author

$M$. *L. Buchman has* over 40 novels in print. His military romantic suspense books have been named Barnes & Noble and NPR "Top 5 of the Year," nominated for the Reviewer's Choice Award for "Top 10 Romantic Suspense of 2014" by RT Book Reviews, and twice Booklist "Top 10 of the Year" placing two of his titles on their "The 101 Best Romance Novels of the Last 10 Years." In addition to romance, he also writes thrillers, fantasy, and science fiction.

In among his career as a corporate project manager he has: rebuilt and single-handed a fifty-foot sailboat, both flown and jumped out of airplanes, designed and built two houses, and bicycled solo around the world.

He is now making his living as a full-time writer on the Oregon Coast with his beloved wife. He is constantly amazed at what you can do with a degree in Geophysics. You may keep up with his writing and receive exclusive content by subscribing to his newsletter at www.mlbuchman.com.

Coming soon, Eagle Cove #3:

# Longing for Eagle Cove
# (excerpt)

*T*his is…*different."* *Natalya Lamont* had been to a number of friends' weddings, but none like this.

"It's Becky after all," her mother agreed. That had them both smiling because in a way that *did* explain everything.

Eagle Cove in mid-winter didn't offer a lot of venues for weddings. A classic January storm was rattling the Oregon Coast hard with intense winds and curtains of lashing rain. That made an outdoor wedding like Jessica's back in the fall out of the question. The Grange Hall had long since been converted into dog kennels and a training area for Catbird Service Assistance Dogs.

Her mom's Victorian B&B had hosted many weddings, but none on this scale. It seemed as if half the town had turned out for Becky.

"Doubt if you'd get a dozen people at my wedding."

Her mother threw her head back and laughed. Gina Lamont had the best laugh, she always gave in to it completely. The people around them joined in with bright smiles even though they couldn't have heard the conversation. Mom's laugh just did that to people.

"You'll have more than that, dear. We'll invite Becky and she'll bring her friends." The big room was packed, so it was hard to argue. And her mother said it in that way of hers that sounded positive and friendly instead of the way Natalya would have said it with a tease and a nudge.

The options had come down to The Flicker movie theater (awkward and nowhere for dancing afterward), Peggy's airplane hangar (which would be bitterly cold), and Becky's barn (which was so much more inviting than that sounded). Over the fifteen years since they'd graduated high school together, she'd converted her father's cow barn into one of the hottest craft-beer breweries on the coast. The cow stalls had been replaced with a giant copper cooking kettle, massive fermenting tanks, a bottling machine, lines of kegs, and all of the other strange and magical equipment that Becky used to practice her art. She'd walled in a part of the upstairs hayloft as an apartment, which was a very cozy space that had everything except a living room.

The living room was on the ground floor and had once been the milk processing room. Becky had converted that into a comfortable sitting area that connected to both the brewery and to the space they were using for the wedding. It was presently a whorl of bridal mayhem. Bridesmaids, best friends, well-meaning wedding guests, and family were all crowded together and hurrying about until finally Natalya and her mom had moved to the entryway into the old calving barn just to be out of the way.

The wedding proper filled the old calving barn to capacity. Becky had fixed it up as a tasting room. She'd refinished the inside wood so that the Douglas fir planking glowed warmly under a wash of indirect lighting. A long oak bar with fifteen beer taps took up one end. It now served as a backdrop for the ceremony.

Behind the bar were lined up a dozen beer taps, from lager at one end to stout at the other. And there was always a pony keg of cream soda or root beer hooked up as well. The taps were all bluebirds for Becky's childhood nickname, with the flavor clearly marked on each bird's wing. Above the bar was a massive painting of the town of Eagle Cove as it would be seen from a plane flying offshore. Oddly it had been painted by both Becky and Peggy, which Natalya decide was only appropriate to today's ceremony. It *was* Becky after all.

To the sides of the long room stood an odd assortment of twenty tables and a hundred chairs that had been borrowed from the diner and other places around town. Because Becky had cleared out the cases of bottled beer usually offered for sale, there was plenty of room for the dancing afterward.

But first there were two weddings to manage.

"Which of us is first again?" Her mom asked, dithering far more than normal. Gina Lamont was a statuesque redhead with an easiness that Natalya had always envied. Yet being bridesmaid to one of her closest friends, Peggy Naron, who had been one of the other long-term single women of the town, had definitely put Mom off her game.

"I go first," Natalya reassured her. "See?" she pointed to the Judge standing in front of the bar at the far end. He was an imposing man even without his black magisterial robes. In them today, with his shock of white hair and somber expression, he looked truly grand. If he was ready, then it was Harry's and Becky's ceremony first.

Jessica arrived in a flurry. She instantly started fussing with the gown that Natalya was wearing (a long black sheath that matched Jessica's), the flowers she was holding (a beautiful bouquet of winter jasmine and red poinsettia that matched Jessica's), and her hair (dark and worn loose past her shoulders, nothing like Jessica's blond layer cut). Finally Natalya had to slap at her hands.

"Stop it, Jessica. Is Becky ready?"

In answer, Tiffany gave them both a light shove from behind and she and Jessica headed up the aisle, making way for Becky, the bride.

There weren't really aisles. Some chairs had been moved to the front to accommodate the elderly, but it was more a friendly gathering than anything organized.

"We're like plowshares," Natalya whispered as the two of them forged a pathway and shooed Emily and Danny's twin girls out of the way.

Jessica did a subtle point and nod in Natalya's direction that as good as said, "You're next!" Which made sense as Natalya was the last of their group.

The three of them had been best friends since, well, birth; and after today she'd be in the unmarried minority instead of the "cheerfully single majority" that they had all proclaimed on and off over the years.

But there wasn't a soul on her horizon. There were always men hanging around, but none of them were interesting enough for more than a dalliance. Jessica was the tall, slender blond, and Becky the short, curvy dark blond; Natalya was the one who had never fit. She was as tall as Jessica, but had the curves her friend had always whined about never developing, without being as lushly figured as Becky. She had hair the color of chestnut and skin the shade of a tropical suntan. Which meant that she looked nothing like her friends, her mother, or the few photos of the man who her mother had dubbed, "That utter disaster." Natalya could barely remember her father's name most of the time. "T.U.D." her mother would say when referring to him until his name might as well be Tud. A missing "r" was always implied by her tone.

There was no more sign of Tud in the crowd than there had been over the last thirty-two years and she didn't miss what she'd never had. Not much anyway. Natalya had never really dreamed about finding a permanent man in her life, but her friends were spoiling that.

The crowd had parted enough that Natalya could now see Harry Slater standing at the head of the aisle, vainly trying to catch a glimpse of his wife-to-be. Becky was six inches shorter than her and Jessica's five-ten, so he'd just have to get a grip and hang on. His brother Greg stood close beside him in his new suit; his eyes were only for his four-months pregnant wife.

"You should be banished," she whispered to Jessica as they neared the head of the aisle.

"Me? What did I do?"

"Looking too damned happy."

"You'll see," was all the frustrating response that her friend offered.

Natalya didn't want to see. She wouldn't mind a man someday, but they'd have to be cut out of a different cloth than any men she'd ever dated.

The third groomsman towered above both brothers and even the Judge.

Cal Mason Jr. was built on as massive a scale as the suit that actually looked damned sharp on him. Cal was the sort of guy you wouldn't think owned a suit but the charcoal gray three-piece looked amazing. He'd crossed six foot in junior high and by the time he and Harry were lead strikers for the Puffin High soccer team, he'd topped out at six-four. He also had a massive frame more appropriate for football, though Natalya could still recall how fleet and agile he'd been as he raced up and down the field. Harry might have thought he'd ruled the games, or that it had been a cooperative effort, but Cal was simply in another league. The problem was that he'd known it.

She could see him joking with Harry, either being shallow, or maybe trying to help keep Harry's nerves in check; it was hard to tell, but she'd bet on the former. The instant Harry spotted the bride, Cal Jr. might as well have been babbling away on some other planet.

He caught on quickly and began scanning the room. His eyes slid past Natalya with as much recognition as—

He jolted and turned back to look at her. Not Jessica. And not Becky. Definitely her.

She made a point of shifting to a preoccupied expression and looking away as if he didn't exist. At least that was the plan. But Cal's attention had riveted on her and she couldn't ignore her reaction to that familiar smile that spread across his features. In fact, Natalya almost bumped into the groom at the head of the aisle by the Judge, because she was having trouble looking away from Cal Jr.

Only when Jessica pinched her, rather more sharply than Natalya felt was called for, did she veer to the bride's side. Even the Judge looked at her a little oddly.

\# \# \#

What the hell was up with weddings?

Cal wanted to ask Harry, but he was all busy with responses, vows, and the biggest shit-eating grin a guy ever wore. Of course, marrying Becky Billings, it was hard to blame the guy. She was damned cute. Wedding white did absolutely nothing to hide how hot the woman was. It also didn't hide that her smile was just as ridiculously oversized as Harry's.

After a bit of debate, Harry had chosen Greg to do the actual best man dance, carrying the ring and all that. It was fine with Cal; nice to see the two brothers getting along for a change. He'd have bet that to last mere minutes after Harry had moved back into town, but whenever they started getting out of hand one of their women stepped in and shut it down. They got along better, so he'd have to admit that was one benefit of marriage. Just an unexpected one.

With nothing much else to do, other than make sure Harry wasn't dumb enough to nerve out at the last moment, Cal had set himself to surveying the crowd.

Not a soul from New Orleans for the groom's side. Man had been a hotshit lawyer down there for a decade and he didn't even have the decency to invite a cute paralegal for Cal. As for the townies who'd shown up, Cal knew every one of them and had dated more than a few. He knew that Emily would give him a dance, but her husband would hog her most of the time. And the way Greg was looking at Jessica, there wouldn't be much cutting in there either.

But even pretending he didn't already know, there was no question where he was going for the first dance. Which took him back to his original question: What the hell was up with weddings?

He'd known Natalya Lamont since before they'd done the old: if you show me yours, I'll show you mine. They'd been six and they'd both chickened. When they were old enough for that question to take on a whole different meaning it had never come up again. She'd blended into the scenery of Eagle Cove until he'd no longer really seen her.

Oh, his hormones had tracked her whenever she'd crossed a room, her and every other girl of their thirty-four person high school class. A field of eighteen women in his senior class yet he'd never so much as touched Natalya.

Then today she'd come walking through the brewery crowd with her dark hair sweeping down over her shoulders and those deep eyes catching the Christmas lights Becky had strung everywhere. If he could ever find someone to explain what it was that happened at weddings, he'd ask them about grown women and "twinkle lights."

As the bride and groom were doing the "Until death do us part" thing, he had to glance over Greg's head to check out what

Natalya had been wearing. Somehow that hadn't even registered as she'd come up the aisle. Just that hair and face and those deep eyes that stared straight back without blinking. It was unnatural how long that woman could go without blinking; like she was casting a spell or something.

Jessica and Natalya wore long black sheath dresses complete with black, paper flower corsages.

He got the joke right away. The death of another life of singlehood. Cute. Damned cute. No, that had described Becky Billings. Cute didn't cover it for long shapely women with smoke-dark eyes.

She'd never looked so…

"You can kiss the bride now, son," Judge Slater told Harry and Cal had missed his chance to mess with the ceremony just to tease his friend. He wasn't low enough to mess with "the moment" for his buddy, but that didn't mean he was above trying to tap in on the first dance.

Though, if he *could* arrange it so that his first dance was with Natalya Lamont, maybe he'd leave Becky Billings and Harry Slater to themselves.

# # #

Rather than the couple returning down the aisle to cheers and congratulations, there was an awkward shuffling that happened, though the applause was generous.

Becky laughed and raced back up the aisle, hiking up her skirts to knee high in her hurry.

Jessica gave Natalya a nudge to remind her of their wedding rehearsal move. The two of them moved aside from the impromptu altar to join the leading edge of the crowd.

Every time Natalya had stolen a glance at the groomsmen, Cal Jr. had been looking at her over the tops of the others' heads. It had unnerved her enough not to join in the happy tears streaming down Jessica's cheeks.

"I'm just being hormonal," Jessica wiped at her face with one hand as the other rested on the slight bulge of her waistline that would have been invisible if the dress weren't so clingy.

"Uh-huh. You're turning into a mush, Jessica Baxter."

"Just wait until it happens to you."

"Not likely." And for perhaps the first time in her life, that answer didn't sit well.

The newly married Harry Slater had stepped up to his father, and Natalya could hear him.

"Okay, Dad. Hand them over."

The Judge actually looked worried. That was a look she'd never seen on his face before. Ever. She'd seen fear when his wife had been dying three years before, but never worry.

Natalya started to look away to see where Cal Jr. was, in order to make sure that he wasn't still staring at her, when Jessica nudged her in the ribs.

"What?"

Jessica just nodded back toward the alter.

Harry actually held his father's hand in a two-handed clasp, a degree of closeness that was still very unusual to see between the two men who'd been estranged for so long.

"You'll do fine, Dad. It's me I'm worried about. What if I screw this up?"

"Son," the Judge's voice rumbled out, carrying easily to where Natalya stood despite the chatting of the crowd anxious for the second ceremony. "You'll do fine. Weddings are one of the very best parts of being a judge."

"Then hand them over," Harry plucked at his father's robe and eased the moment with a smile.

Judge Slater had served over thirty years on the bench before retiring to cook at the local diner and hold office hours in the afternoon. Harry had just been elected to his father's judicial seat in November and was now fully instated.

The room slowly fell silent as Judge John Slater removed his robes and helped Judge Harry Slater don and settle them.

When it was complete, the two men embraced. Natalya glanced aside and saw that she wasn't the only one crying. She and Jessica leaned against each other for support.

"Now, get over there," Harry gave his father a gentle shove until the Judge was standing where Harry had, just moments before. Cal Sr., almost as big as his son and nearly as imposing as the Judge, came up to shake John's hand and thump him on the shoulder. Greg stepped back to the altar and shook his father's hand as well before he and Cal Sr. stepped to the side.

Someone started the music and Natalya turned to look back down the aisle. This time it was her mother and Becky who were "plowing" the aisle clear for the bride, and the two judges were both rapt.

Natalya couldn't see Peggy in her wedding white except as a flurry of dark red hair just visible over Becky's head.

But she could most certainly see the way that Cal Mason Jr. was watching her from across the aisle.

*Available soon at fine retailers everywhere*

# Other works by M. L. Buchman:

<u>Angelo's Hearth</u>
*Where Dreams are Born*
*Where Dreams Reside*
*Maria's Christmas Table*
*Where Dreams Unfold*
*Where Dreams Are Written*

<u>Eagle Cove</u>
*Return to Eagle Cove*
*Recipe for Eagle Cove*

<u>The Night Stalkers</u>
*The Night Is Mine*
*I Own the Dawn*
*Daniel's Christmas*
*Wait Until Dark*
*Frank's Independence Day*
*Peter's Christmas*
*Take Over at Midnight*
*Light Up the Night*
*Christmas at Steel Beach*
*Bring On the Dusk*
*Target of the Heart*
*Target Lock on Love*
*Christmas at Peleliu Cove*
*Zachary's Christmas*
*By Break of Day*

<u>Firehawks</u>
*Pure Heat*
*Wildfire at Dawn*
*Full Blaze*
*Wildfire at Larch Creek*
*Wildfire on the Skagit*
*Hot Point*
*Flash of Fire*

<u>Delta Force</u>
*Target Engaged*

<u>Deities Anonymous</u>
*Cookbook from Hell: Reheated*
*Saviors 101*

<u>Thrillers</u>
*Swap Out!*
*One Chef!*
*Two Chef!*

<u>SF/F Titles</u>
*Nara*
*Monk's Maze*